RAWHIDE RIDER

"Get 'em out to the barn," the outlaw leader said. "We'll leave our calling card."

Brad and the girl watched as Sam and Ezra were tied to stanchions in the barn. They failed to understand till Wells climbed to the loft and kicked down a quantity of hay. It was piled against the wall in the corner, and Harve dug out a match.

"What are you doing?" Letty screamed. "Harve Wells, that's murder!"

Wells grinned as he lit the hay.

A POWDER VALLEY WESTERN

RAWHIDE RIDER

PETER FIELD

AVON BOOKS ◆ NEW YORK

AVON BOOKS
A division of
The Hearst Corporation
105 Madison Avenue
New York, New York 10016

First Avon Books Printing: October 1989

AVON TRADEMARK REG. U.S. PAT. OFF. AND IN OTHER COUNTRIES, MARCA
REGISTRADA, HECHO EN U.S.A.

Printed in the U.S.A.

K–R   10   9   8   7   6   5   4   3   2   1

1.

IN STRONG AFTERNOON SUNLIGHT a tall, hawk-nosed, scare-crow figure of a man drew rein on the crest of a mesquite garnished ridge to gaze anxiously toward the ranch sprawled out in the valley below. He was red haired and no longer young, with a battered flat-crown sombrero perched on the side of his head, and a black patch shielding the socket of one missing eye, which lent him a decidedly rakish aspect.

His companion, a stocky, bull-necked person garbed in tattered bib-overalls, so fat that his stubby legs jutted out uncomfortably, gave the ranch little more than a sour glance.

"Yuh reckon we'll find the old skinflint home, Ez?" he growled.

The lanky man grunted fiercely. "We'll either find him home—or he won't find that ranch when he gets back," he retorted.

For a moment they delayed, scanning the apparently lifeless ranch with narrow attention. This was the moder-ately prosperous Rafter A, a dozen miles northwest of Powder Valley, Colorado; its owner, Rafe Alford, a noto-rious pinch-penny and shrewd dealer, was reputedly rich. From the thoroughly disreputable look of these newcom-ers, they might have been raiders in the act of planning a treacherous attack.

Their actions, however, soon belied any such interpretation for they shoved their horses into motion and jogged straight down the slope in plain sight, making directly for the ranch yard. Not a soul put in an appearance as they approached.

Determinedly gnawing his ragged fringe of mustache, the tall man leaned from his saddle and pounded on the sagging kitchen door. There was no response. His stocky friend rasped the blue-black stubble covering his pendulous jaw and stared about in scowling perplexity.

"Wouldn't put it past the old coot t' be hidin' on us," he muttered. "Trouble is—where?"

The other was obviously not interested in fruitless discussion, sliding from the saddle in a single long step. "Come on," he rumbled peremptorily. "We'll spread out an' comb this dump good!"

With a half-groan, the stout man dismounted and started to circle the house, examining its windows with an eagle eye. Crossing the back and coming to the farther corner, he paused, his glance caught. In the direction of the corrals his companion stood before the open door of a tumble-down shed, his hands on his hips. He had found something.

"What yuh got, Ez?" the pudgy man asked as he hastened forward. He halted beside the other, to find Rafe Alford, the Rafter A owner, inside the shed fumbling busily with a snarl of leather straps.

Hearing the scuff of boots, Alford glanced up absently. "That you, Ezra? . . . Howdy, Sloan." Nodding, he went on with his work.

Ezra and Sam Sloan exchanged a wordless glance. It was a moment before the former spoke. "If yuh can spare a minute, we'd like t' talk to yuh," he announced with scarcely concealed sarcasm.

"Yeh—sure," grunted Alford, tugging away fiercely. "But yuh can wait till I get this done, I expect!"

A long minute dragged by, Sloan watching him with increasing curiosity. "What is that yuh got there, Rafe?"

Alford held up a patched and riveted headgear long past its prime. "It's a crime, the stuff that's wasted round here," he grumbled discontentedly. "My foreman tossed this bridle out, claimin' it kept bustin' on him—but it'll do *me* for a while and I can save my own."

Sam gazed at him admiringly. "That's the ticket," he assented readily. "Save a dollar, an' yuh'll never want one, I always say."

Ezra could be heard breathing noisily. His homely horse-face showed his blistering scorn for this rancher who could afford silver-mounted bridles without even straining his pocketbook. Somehow, however, he managed to control his feelings.

"That's fine, Alford." His tone was a rasp. "No doubt a forward-lookin' hombre like you is prepared t' pay us for the herd of roan horses we delivered two months ago!"

Rafe glared at him. For an instant his breath appeared to catch. "Ain't gettin' in a sweat, are yuh?" he barked testily.

"We don't reckon we are." Sloan's drawl was smooth. "A sixty-day note is one thing, Alford. This was supposed t' be a sale for cash."

Rafe was listening now with averted eye. "Told yuh I wanted t' make sure them roans was as represented," he grumbled sulkily.

"Oh sure. But nothin' was said about makin' them earn themselves before we're paid," rumbled Ezra. Partners in the Bar ES horse ranch in Powder Valley, during the summer he and Sloan had sold Alford in the neighborhood of a hundred head of prime roan horses. It was fall now—high time they were fingering their hard-earned profits.

But Rafe was stubborn. "Well—I don't aim t' get stuck!" he insisted.

Sam reasoned with him patiently. "Look, Alford. You asked for time, and we give yuh a month. You took two. Even you'll agree this has got t' end somewhere—"

Rafe appeared almost too scared to discuss it rationally. Dread lurked in his scowl. He hated to part with money, even when he knew he must. Ezra let him run on for a while, before his patience came to an end.

"Forget it, then." He was sternly curt. "We wouldn't think o' forcin' yuh to buy. We can unload that poor stock somewhere else in a jiffy." He was being sarcastic again. "Me and Sam'll just round up them roans and drive 'em on home—"

"Hang it, Ezra! You can't do that. I'm right in the middle of roundup," blurted Rafe. "Even hired me some extra hands for a week. I can't spare the roans now."

Ezra had shrewdly guessed as much. He shook his head, not removing the pressure for an instant. "Too bad. Reckon we'll want our horses before they're all ganted up—"

Alford found this threatened catastrophe too much to

withstand. He really needed the roans, which had already proved themselves excellent animals. "Well—maybe I could make out to give yuh a small deposit," he proposed craftily.

"Maybe yuh could let us have them broncs back, too!" Ez let him have both barrels now. "You darned tightwad— what kind o' blazer are you tryin' to run on us, anyhow?" he roared.

Rafe abruptly wilted before this blast. "Don't get nervous, Ezra," he urged. "I'll go in the house and see how much I can spare." Propelled by the big redhead's parting shot, he scuttled toward the ranch house, slamming the door behind him.

"That did it." Ezra masked a dour grin. "He's aimin' t' shake the moths out of that money finally. It comes hard—"

About to reply, Sam paused to glance around as a handful of hard-bitten punchers rode up to the Rafter A corrals. "Rafe's extra hands," he grunted under his breath, looking them over.

Dismounting and turning their dust-caked broncs in, the cowboys stared at them without offering to speak. Rafe emerged from the house a moment later. He stumped forward, his face curiously set.

Before Alford opened his mouth, Ezra knew he was primed for further delaying tactics. But Sloan had spotted the sheaf of greenbacks in the rancher's fist. He pitched into Alford vigorously, and they argued heatedly before the rancher could bring himself to hand over the money.

Bitter as he found the task, Alford was counting the full amount for the roans into Ezra's broad palm when a cool and guttural voice broke into the talk.

"Nice wad of jack there, boys. I won't ask what you're aiming to do with it!"

They looked up, startled, into the expressionless face of a brazen, level-eyed fellow who made no bones of stepping forward directly into their midst. He was one of Alford's temporary hands, his companions not far behind him.

Rafe stared blankly, flushing red. "Get up fresh ponies, Wells," he ordered sharply. "And get back to the roundup ground—"

The man called Wells reached out and snatched the wad of bills from Ezra before the latter could make a move. Ez's eye leaped, and then fixed, as he saw several guns trained on them from less than a dozen feet away. Sam saw it too, and his bristly jaw hung ajar.

"Of all the danged gall——" he began in a choked voice.

Wells coolly turned and slapped him hard with his free hand. He had not bothered to draw his own weapon, but his chill eyes were like two knives.

"Shut up, lard head," he rasped carelessly.

Sam opened his lips, and then closed them without speaking. The look in his eyes said that he was by no means intimidated; but he knew when he was up against a tough proposition. Wells watched him with a lurking, ruthless half-smile, and tucked the money into his pants pocket.

"Blast it, Harve! You'll never get away with——" Alford began an angry protest, which died under the puncher's chilling glance.

"Wrong again, Rafe," retorted Wells coolly. "From the time we come here I suspected you must have a bundle——but this is the first time I've seen any of it," he said cynically. "We'll call it our pay, since we won't be waitin' . . . Doc." He turned to address one of his confederates. "You and Gila scare up some rope. We'll just put these brave hombres out of circulation, for a while anyhow."

Rafe Alford sputtered angrily while his hands were being bound behind him; and if looks could kill, Sloan would have come out a sure winner. Ezra had as yet spoken no word, nor did he now; but the unblinking glint of his single shrewd eye did not escape Harve Wells's notice.

"Do a job on this string bean," he told his fellows curtly. "He's lookin' us over like he expected to see us again!"

Ezra's long arms were yanked behind him with unnecessary force, and pain twitched across his rugged face as they brutally tripped him and bound his legs as securely. The trio were quickly trussed up and tumbled into a corner of the shed.

"You're makin' a mistake, Harve," warned Gila as the renegades turned away.

"Don't reckon I am," retorted Wells dryly. "There'll be a line on us anyhow when we turn up missin'. A murder rap would only make it hotter." Whatever he might have added was lost as they moved beyond earshot.

Silence descended on the shed, broken only by Ezra's heavy puffing. "You all right, Ez?" Sam blurted, trying to roll over.

"Sure, I'm fine!" Ezra exploded angrily. "You oughta know that. Ain't a thing in the world botherin' me!!"

"Well—yuh got your breath anyhow." Sam sounded injured. "Didn't know but what yuh might be chokin'—"

"And hopin' I was, no doubt!" snarled Ez.

But his testiness was only the measure of his exasperation, and they began planning their escape at once. Ezra was quick to see that salvation lay in their not having been bound immovably to center-posts, as might have been done. Rolling back to back, they had a few inches play with their cramped fingers. The tall redhead's had already grown numb, and Sloan's were in little better condition.

Giving up Ezra's iron knots after a twenty-minute trial, Sam rolled over to Alford, grunting and puffing. He succeeded at last in freeing Rafe's legs; after which they found themselves in little better case. Livid about the gills, Alford looked all but demoralized by his manhandling. Ezra lay glaring at him in disgust.

"Dammit, Rafe! Get up on your hocks," he bellowed. "Yuh can manage that much."

Electrified by this wrath, the rancher struggled violently and presently staggered to his feet.

"Now work your wrists against that scythe standin' in the corner," commanded Ezra.

Rafe caught on fast. But he was clumsy. He cut himself and swore. Five minutes later his bonds fell apart. He was free. "All right—now turn us loose," Sam broke in shortly. "Shake it up, man! Them buzzards've already got half an hour's start on us."

Alford fumbled at their bonds in haste, finally managing to release them. Sam heaved to his feet with a growl. Ezra staggered and fell back.

"Get the broncs, Sam," he muttered. "While I work the blood back into my hands and legs—"

Sam hurried from the shed, glancing keenly about. He need not have worried: the Rafter A was once more completely deserted. For a moment he thought Wells had driven their own horses off, before he found them quietly cropping grass along a pasture fence.

Ez was standing before the shed when Sam brought the ponies forward. "Come on, Alford—get goin'," he barked. "Dig some guns out o' that rat's nest o' yours while we snag yuh a bronc. We're takin' after them blacklegs an' not wastin' any time about it!"

Though their arms had been confiscated, his tone was belligerent. Rafe appeared after some delay with a .45 and a battered carbine. Sam produced a spare Colt from his saddlebag; and he and Ezra had snaked a bronc from the corral for Rafe.

Ez took charge as they set out without talk. He was a tracker without peer in this part of the country despite the handicap to his sight. Before they had gone five miles he picked up the sign of Wells and his men, solving without effort a clumsy attempt or two by the renegades to conceal their tracks.

The trail led west into the wild heights of the Culebra range. It had been midafternoon when they approached the Rafter A, and the sun soon dropped behind the lofty mountains. The shadows lengthened. Working deeper into the lonely hills, Ezra led the way into rugged and treacherous Snake Canyon as the light began to fail. Unquestionably the outlaws had come this way. Their tracks ran on, to disappear in the shallow waters of Cache Creek. They did not reappear on the other bank. Sam Sloan glanced about the gloomy, pine-choked defile.

"Question is—did they turn upstream, or down?"

As always while working out a range problem, Ezra was almost indifferent. "Mornin' may tell—"

Rafe caught at that. "Yuh mean we gotta lay out here overnight? . . . Unh-uh." He was vehement. "Not me, Ezra. I got to get back to the roundup."

"An' miss the chance of snaggin' them skunks?" rasped Ez bluntly.

"Well—it means more t' you, I'll admit," returned Rafe lamely. "I'll remind yuh I paid for them roans. It's *you* them hombres robbed—took it right out of your hand, if yuh ain't forgot!''

It was true enough. But Ezra's contempt knew no bounds on being reminded of this. For all his hot words he was unable to alter Alford's decision; but the rancher rode away into gathering darkness, giving up the chase, with burning ears.

Pitching camp where they were, Ezra and Sam were astir with the first streaks of dawn the following morning. All day they diligently combed the environs of Snake Canyon without laying eyes on the renegades' vanished trail.

"Hang it, Ez—we're gettin' no place fast," complained Sam bitterly. His grudge against Harvey Wells and his crowd had grown personal since Alford's defection.

"If yuh think yuh can do better, go ahead!" Ezra fired up testily. For once, however, Sam did not take offense at his tone.

"No—I'm thinkin' of Pat," the stocky man returned slowly. "He'd want to be in this. An' I aim t' tell him.''

He was speaking of Pat Stevens, their closest friend, and owner of the Lazy Mare Ranch in Powder Valley. The younger man had dragged them out of many a jam in the past; and while Sloan could scarcely be got to admit as much, he was remembering it now. Ezra's reception of the proposal to call on Stevens was evident in his prompt response.

"Let's get about it, then." He turned his horse.

The truth was, hunger made them relinquish the pursuit as much as anything. Going without food was not one of the things they did best. Two hours later, accordingly, they rode into the Lazy Mare yard to find Stevens and his sour-faced handyman, Crusty Hodge, conferring on the ranch house porch.

"Get the griddle hot, you," Ezra called to Hodge without ceremony. "Stevens, come here an' listen t' this!"

Pat came out, obviously deeply curious. The pair blurted their story indignantly, wrapped up in their wrongs, and so engrossed that they were keenly startled when a deep voice broke in on them, directed coldly at Stevens.

"Here yuh are, Wells." The words dropped flatly.

"Looks like I caught up with you and a couple of your pals!"

They whirled to meet the unwavering eyes of a burly man who wore the star of a United States marshal on his chest. A slit-eyed, heavily armed deputy sat his saddle a few paces behind him, alert and waiting.

2.

"HOWDY, MARSHAL." Broad-shouldered and clean-cut of face, Pat Stevens revealed no trace of feeling, his gray eyes steady and friendly. "Stevens is the name. Don't believe I've ever met you before."

"Gif Towner, they call me," the lawman murmured. "You shouldn't have any difficulty rememberin' that—"

Shaking his head, Pat looked politely puzzled. "I don't, though."

Towner looked skeptical. "Well, *I* ain't troubled that way—regardless of the name you're travelin' under just now."

"Hold on, here!" Sam glanced from the marshal to Pat, and back again. "I heard what yuh called him—" He began to laugh incredulously. "Don't tell me yuh got *him* mixed up in your head with Harve Wells!"

By no means impressed, Towner continued to gaze unwaveringly at Pat. "Names come unstuck mighty easy in this country."

Ezra's gruff chuckle broke in. "But dang it, Marshal! What're yuh drivin' at, anyhow? This *is* Pat Stevens. He owns this ranch. Anybody'll tell yuh that!"

"I'm not disputin' his—present identity." Gif Towner was curt. "But I've seen Harve Wells's picture, too." There was clearly a menace in his inference.

"Harve Wells is some owlhoot, I take it," Pat interrupted, quietly insistent. "What makes you so sure I'm him?"

"Simple. I know what Wells looks like. He looks like you. I got the story from Rafe Alford this mornin' of how he was robbed. Picked up the outlaws' trail, and followed it straight here," said Towner flatly. "And here you are!"

Ezra's face congested. "Yuh follered *our* trail here," he bawled. "We're the pair that was robbed, man, after Rafe paid us for our horses! We trailed Wells till we lost him, an' come after Stevens here. *He* didn't know a thing about it, till we just told him! Of all the crazy, blunderin'—"

"Chop that talk." Towner's powerful jaw snapped like a steel trap. "It don't go with me, but yuh can try it on the judge . . ."

"No need of getting excited about this," broke in Pat calmly. "But Ezra happens to be tellin' the truth, Marshal. I can account for my movements all day," he added.

"No doubt." Towner waved this away. "Only too well, I dare say."

Pat argued with him mildly, presently becoming aware that Sam Sloan was staring at him queerly. "Yes—what is it, Sam?" he queried briefly.

"Danged if yuh *don't* look a little somethin' like Wells at that, Stevens," exclaimed the stocky man with amusement. "Don't tell me at this late date that yuh been leadin' a double life—!"

It was obvious in the hard features of Gif Towner that this was precisely the marshal's own suspicion, without any faint hint of joking about it. Glancing swiftly from face to face, Pat shrugged.

"If true, that's my hard luck." He smiled. "Or should I say Harve Wells's?"

Studying him attentively, Towner relaxed perceptibly for the first time. "A casual likeness is no unheard-of thing," he conceded. "I will say yuh don't seem to resemble Wells too much around the mouth, Stevens."

It was the first time he had used Pat's name. If he was softening, Ezra did not propose to leave it at that. "What's more, Towner, Harve's got smoky brown eyes—as you'll find out, if yuh ever stop wastin' time," he spoke up quickly.

Towner's stern pupils glinted. "Wouldn't swear I'm altogether wastin' it, right here," he retorted bleakly. "I've run into some good actors before now—not that I think you two are concealin' much."

Pat took time to question the partners in more detail about their experience. Only a victim of inveterate suspicion could have questioned their sincere indignation. Regardless of Marshal Towner's course, they felt that they were wasting their own time, and expressed themselves loudly to that effect.

Crusty Hodge appeared at the kitchen door just then. "Grub's on," he muttered, with a resentful glance for Ezra.

Pat nodded. "Get down, Marshal—you and your deputy. Maybe we can get to the bottom of this while we eat. There's not much to be done before morning anyhow."

Towner did not hesitate to accept the invitation. His dour expression said, however, that it would prove uphill work to alter his fixed opinion unless they came up with more than he had heard as yet. As it turned out, an incident soon occurred which could scarcely have been better designed to support Stevens.

Talk was still sparing while they dulled the first keen edge of hunger when the door swung open and a man entered. It was Johnson, Pat's foreman. Paying no heed to the others present, he addressed a blunt question to Stevens concerning the ranch work. Pat replied briefly by outlining the next day's work, recommending that a certain herd of steers be culled for the fall market.

"Yuh mean that stock yuh helped us shove down onto winter range this afternoon?" queried Johnson.

A few more words passed, to which Gif Towner listened with cocked eyebrow. Johnson could scarcely have been aware that his employer badly needed an alibi for his whereabouts during the day. Having casually produced one without knowing it, the foreman turned to depart.

"Hold on, Zeke," Pat was good-humored. "You're here. Sit and eat with us."

Johnson declined, with gruff thanks. "I'll get back to the boys, Stevens." He left.

No reference was made to the exchange as empty plates were shoved back. Pat rolled a smoke and licked it shut, lifting a bland eye to the lawman's face. "Still of the same mind about me, Towner?"

A less accomplished poker hand might have given himself away at this moment. The marshal only shrugged stolidly. "What've yuh got to offer?" he countered.

Pat hunched forward. "It sticks in my mind what Sam says about my lookin' like this Wells. You seem to think I do too. It gives me an idea . . . What if I was to make a stab at joinin' this owlhoot crowd, with a view to turnin' them over to the law? Not," he grinned quickly, "as a concession to your unworthy suspicions, you understand! But these boys are friends of mine. I'd be willing to go that far on the chance of gettin' their money back—"

"Sa-ay!" It was a new idea to Sloan, and one he wholeheartedly approved. "You've hit it, Stevens! All three of us'll go. O' course, Ez and I can't hope to get in with the gang themselves—they'd recognize us—but we can sure make things hot for 'em."

But it was Towner's endorsement for which Pat waited. The lawman pursed his lips deliberately. "Well, it'll alter my opinion of yuh considerable, Stevens, if you'd tackle it," he ventured, only to resume cautiously: "On the other hand, if my first hunch was right—" He broke off significantly.

Pat chuckled. "That's the chance you take. But let's not kid ourselves. You're up against a rough proposition, Towner. You wouldn't want it said you'd brought in the wrong man . . . I'm offerin' to help. And I *do* own this spread, amounting to a considerable outlay. Would I risk it all for the few thousand dollars stolen from my best friends?"

It was not uncommon for a law enforcement officer to appear remarkably obtuse when it suited his best interests. In the face of Pat's persuasive argument, Towner only looked dubious.

"I ain't in the habit of decidin' things in a hurry," he stated frankly. "Your offer is either mighty reasonable—or awful smart. I'll sleep on it, Stevens. I suppose I can make myself at home?"

"You don't want me to say I'm glad you're here." Pat's smile was disarming. "But I'll endeavor to bear up under it. Crusty can dig up any amount of blankets in a pinch, Towner. Help yourself."

No one pretended to ignore the constraint forced on them by the situation. But Stevens spent the evening ex- actly as he would have done in Towner's absence; and after uninhibited discussion of the robbery with Ezra and Sam, yawned his way to bed at an early hour.

Crusty woke them all in the morning, rattling the stove-lids before daylight. Breakfast awaited as soon as they dressed and stamped into their boots. Little was said as they ate, but Gif Towner's announcement of his decision, when it came, was markedly undramatic.

"Aim to get started right off, I expect, Stevens?"

Pat's nod was as casual. "We may lose some time pickin' up Wells's trail. If he's pullin' out of the country it could turn into a long ride."

"He won't be—no fear o' that." Sloan spoke up unexpectedly.

"How do yuh figure that?" Towner pounced on him in a flash. But Sam had no more to say, nor would any amount of needling move him to explain.

"Well." Stevens picked up his saddle. "We're off, boys." He let Sam and Ezra precede him into the open, and paused. "I suppose I can contact yuh somewhere here in Powder Valley, Towner?"

Gif would not commit himself. "Any law officer can get in touch with me, Stevens. Get somethin' first on these owlhoots and we'll see."

Pat left it at that. Riding away from the Lazy Mare a few minutes later with Ezra and Sam, he found the situation ironically amusing. "I've been accused of a variety of shady dealin's in the past." His glance rested lightly on the pair. "Now it's got down to havin' to prove myself innocent first."

Ezra stared at him sharply. "Just what do yuh draw from that?" he demanded suspiciously.

Pat shrugged. "Don't know, unless you and Sam's looks are against us. All too often I'm charged with the company I keep—"

He ducked the wild pass aimed at his hat by Ezra, and quickly sobered. "What made you so sure Harve Wells won't leave the country, Sam?" he asked.

"I could be wrong—but Rafe Alford is awful tight." Sloan was dogged. "Don't forget that Wells was a Rafter A hand . . . Mebby Rafe figured out a way t' get us paid off without losin' his money," he suggested craftily. "He give up the chase awful easy. Could be they're all laughin' at us right now.''

Pat thought that over and shook his head. "You've got a low mind, Sam. You or Ez might try that gag in a pinch," he said. "Rafe wouldn't have the guts.''

Sam muttered discontentedly but said no more.

Pat led the way to Snake Canyon, and Ezra pointed out where they had lost the tracks of the gang. Without moving from his position, Stevens surveyed their gloomy surroundings with care. "Fairly sure they turned up the creek, or down, Ez?" he mused.

"Ain't sure o' nothin,'' was the crabbed response.

Humming under his breath, Pat splashed his pony across and examined the other bank. Sam noticed that he was paying more attention to the breaks in the canyon's rim than to the soil underfoot. After a moment Pat headed for a great rock bordering the water a hundred feet below the ford. It was thickly clumped with alder on one side; and scarcely had Stevens disappeared behind the rock when they heard him call.

Hurrying that way, they were astonished to find the younger man bent over several sets of horse tracks which plainly emerged from the alder clump and continued up the rough canyon slope toward a rocky gap above.

"Where were you lookin' for these tracks when you lost 'em?" Pat inquired mischievously.

The redheaded tracker's face was a picture of chagrin. "Danged if I ain't as dumb as them fellers was,'' ejaculated Ez. "I figured 'em to be playin' it smart while they had the chance. I outsmarted myself—''

Sam had his own salty comment to make. As shrewd a reader of trails as he was, Ezra did not often let them down; that he was not perfect Sloan did not propose to forget. They set off on the recovered trail, bickering hotly till Stevens finally put an end to it.

"By your tell, Wells has got a thirty-hour start," he reminded them shortly. "If we hope to overhaul them we better get about it.''

From that point onward they had no serious trouble in following the sign of the outlaws. The way led deep into the Culebras, and for a time Pat thought that Wells was surely making for the sanctuary of the back ranges, where a man could lose himself for months. After midday, however, they came across the remains of a fire where the outlaws had obviously camped overnight. That Wells had lingered long here was obvious. The trail thereafter appeared considerably fresher.

Moreover, instead of driving on west into ever deeper wilderness, the tracks curved north across a wild mountain flank and once more swung east. The sun was still high in the sky when they found themselves once more riding toward Powder Valley.

"Told yuh Wells wouldn't be leavin' this range, didn't I?" Sam could not resist reminding triumphantly.

"We haven't disputed that," answered Pat serenely. "But there's just the little difference of opinion as to the reason why—"

"So what's your opinion?" challenged the stocky little man.

Pat shrugged. "Don't know. I'm one who's willin' to wait and find out."

Working down into moderately open country once more, after hours of threading the jackstraw down-timber, they made better time. Before long they were watching ahead keenly, aware that they might come upon the quarry without notice. Stevens appeared to grow careless of clinging closely to the signs they followed, and began cutting across loops in the trail where Wells and his fellows had gone out of their way to stick to cover.

Ezra was more methodical. Irked by his previous blunder, he was making doggedly sure that he was not again fooled by the renegades; and Sam was sticking close at his heels.

The time came when Pat drew farther and farther ahead of the pair, and Sloan grew uneasy, gazing after the other. "What's wrong with the zany?" he fretted aloud. "Why don't he stay back here with us? We're liable t' bust onto Wells's crowd any minute—an' there ain't a word been said about how we're goin' to pass ourselves off as owlhoots!"

Ezra was scowling. "Maybe he's got some idea in his head. We can't just ride up an' say we're crooks," he groused sagely.

"Who in hell said we could?" Sam's increasing apprehension was setting his nerves on edge. "This Wells is one

tough cooky—he's got to be t' stay in this business . . .
Hey, Stevens!'' he lifted his voice in a wrathy bellow,
glaring after Pat, who by now was several hundred yards
in the lead and drawing away from them by the minute.

Ezra whirled on his beefy partner angrily. ''Let off
another yowl like that an' I'll bat yuh one, yuh scatterbrained
lug!'' he ripped out fiercely.

Sam glowered his surprise. ''What's eatin' yuh?''

''What's eatin' me!'' Ezra was scathing. ''If Wells is
within three mile he heard that screech—''

Sam was only half attentive. ''Come on.'' He kicked his
bronc into a run. ''It's Stevens that's off his rocker. We're
catchin' up with him right now!''

No less concerned for their friend than Sam, Ez gave an
explosive curse and hurled his horse forward. They had
scarcely burst through a clump of brush into the open, pelting
after Pat at top speed, when to their consternation Stevens
whipped out his .45 and deliberately fired backwards in their
direction.

Sam's incredulous amazement exploded in a loud yell.
''What's the matter with him? He *has* gone nuts!'' he gasped.

Next moment a string of horsemen burst from a fringe
of pines not far beyond Stevens and swept forward. Their
guns glinted and puffs of smoke drifted across the brush.
Not at Pat were they directing their fire, however. Stevens'
slugs had sailed high over the partners' heads; but these
droned so close that Ezra wheeled his pony violently across
Sam's path, crowding him to one side.

''Take cover, Sam!'' he cried sharply. *''That's Wells's
outfit!''*

''Let go o' my bridle,'' raged Sam. ''They got Stevens,
ain't they? I'm pilin' into that bunch like a wet wolf!''

''Lay off, yuh fool!'' blazed Ez in a scornful roar.
''Don't yuh get it? Pat's pulled a trick on us! He's got next
t' Harve Wells at our expense—by pretendin' we're a
posse on his tail—an' I guess that settles it.'' He yanked
his horse about, intent only on immediate flight as the
lethal slugs whined between them and underneath their
ponies, clipping the brush.

With set, despairing face Sam followed suit.

3.

"THANKS, BOYS. I expect that'll do the trick."

Pat's cool talk turned the outlaws back as Sam and Ezra disappeared hastily over a rise. One of the renegades, whom Pat instantly took to be Harve Wells, drifted toward him warily.

"Who are those birds, you?"

"Couple of ranch hands who disputed my title to this bronc." Pat's tone was brazenly amused. "I'll admit I ain't had it long myself. How do I know they wasn't tryin' to steal it?"

He was in fact mounted at the moment on a Bar ES roan, purchased earlier in the season from the partners. Wells took the horse in briefly and scrutinized Pat with some sharpness.

"So what now, friend?" It was an unmistakable challenge.

Pat shrugged. "I'll be shovin' on, I suppose," he let drop. "That is, unless you boys happen to be goin' my way—"

He took Wells's measure critically as he spoke. There was no denying the superficial resemblance between them. Stevens could not tell whether Harve Wells got it or not, but the outlaw leader's manner was frankly suspicious.

"What way would that be?" he asked narrowly.

Pat's grin would have completely disarmed any man less hard. "Most any direction—away from here," he confessed coolly. "Where you headin'?"

"Oh—let him drift along with us, Harve," one of the other men spoke up. "Yuh can chew it over later—if there's anything to discuss."

That Wells was acutely conscious of being near to the

18

scene of the recent robbery was obvious in his curt manner. The outlaw cast watchful glances this way and that, and it was a question whether he distrusted most the stranger in their midst, or the unseen menace which surrounded them every minute they remained in the country.

In the face of this, Pat thought it strange that the owlhoots had deliberately returned to Powder Valley once they had, as they thought, shaken off pursuit.

No trace of Sam and Ezra was seen again, and their single pursuer presently jogged back to join the gang. Pat lost no time turning in with the others as they pushed on. They seemed to know where they were going, making for a miniature badlands in the hills not many miles from the Rafter A. The knowledge gave rise to lively conjecture in Stevens's mind. Was it possible that they entertained further designs on Rafe Alford? Pat would have given something to know; but he avoided calling attention to himself by asking any questions.

The outlaws led the way over winding trails to a sheltered camp situated in a rocky gulch. So secluded and difficult of access was this spot that Pat concluded it had been marked for use while the gang was punching cows for Alford.

One of the outlaws, a grizzled oldtimer called Gila, soon had a fire going. From a shallow cave near at hand he tumbled forth several canvas-covered packs and whipped together a meal of sorts. Pat did not overlook the significance of the cache. Evidently this whole operation had been carefully planned before hand.

The men wolfed down the singed steaks sliced from a quarter of beef. Not till they had gulped down scalding coffee and were building after-supper cigarets was any breath wasted on speech.

A man with a clipped spade beard, who appeared to be of indefinably more refined breeding than the others, glanced across the fire at Wells. "Well, Harve. We backed yuh up there at old Alford's." His calculating tone was suggestive. "How about a divvy of that fat roll the danged tightwad coughed up—"

"Yeh." Gila looked up with brightening interest. "That's right. Reckon we'd all like the chance to finger our own cut!"

Wells appeared flustered, and darted restless looks about the circle. "Careful of your talk, you two." He jerked his head meaningfully in Pat's direction. From his air of frowning impatience, he would have been glad to stop all discussion of the proceeds from Alford's robbery.

Chet Denton, a middleaged, clean-shaven pine knot of a man, regarded Wells sourly. "What do yuh mean?" he barked truculently. "Is this notice that we'll be workin' for nothin', Wells—or what?"

Harve flushed. He was having trouble controlling his temper. "Told you to watch out what yuh say in front of this hombre, didn't I?" He indicated Stevens bluntly.

The outlaws whirled to consider Pat afresh. At the time of his joining them, they had appeared to make up their minds he was their kind. But now, with leisure in which to weigh pros and cons, their baleful stares were not easy to ignore.

Gila advanced on Pat with forceful intent. "We'll settle this here an' now," he growled. "What would your name be, friend, an' just who are yuh?"

Pat had been waiting for some time for this moment. His demeanor was cool, as if he found nothing unusual afoot, or else was perfectly aware of how he meant to handle it.

"Stevens is the name," he murmured, preferring to take the chance of its meaning nothing in particular to them. "I reckon who I happen to be'll have to speak for itself." He seemed almost bored. "I've been through this before, Gila. Pick out which one of you I'll be forced to flatten before you make up your minds to lay off, and we'll get this over with—like you say."

Taken aback by the chill drone in his voice, they regarded him in momentary silence. Then Brad MacEwen, the youngest man of the five, broke the spell with a laugh.

"There you are, Gila! *You've* heard that kind of talk before too, I'll wager." He spoke with assurance. "That ought to satisfy even you he's no hombre to tangle with—"

Hard-bitten as he was, Gila's expression was one of scowling doubt. Certainly he did not intend to accept Pat's careless challenge; nor did the others appear anxious to try conclusions with this stalwart fellow. But Wells was following the conversation alertly, and now he stepped forward.

"*I* ain't satisfied—no matter what the rest of yuh think."
He clipped the words off severely. "A fist-fight won't
convince me this bird is to be trusted, no matter who
wins."

Hot-tempered in his own right, Gila whirled on the
authoritative leader. "What're yuh suggestin' then," he
rifled belligerently. "That I heave him out?"

That gave Harve pause. A wary wolf-look flashed over
his hard face. Obviously he thought Pat knew too much
about them already to be allowed unquestioned freedom.
Pat saved him the necessity of dealing with this problem
by speaking up coldly.

"That does it. I *was* thinkin' of going on my way. I
know Harve didn't take a shine to me . . . But if there's a
question of what I can or can't do, I'll settle it my own
way. I'm stayin'. Now, anyway."

Wells met him eye to eye measuringly at this uncompro-
mising ultimatum. Every man present knew what it spelled.
Both were armed. If Harve seriously meant to register his
protest, now was the time to do it.

Once more MacEwen broke the tension with his drawl.
"Shucks. We're all worn down, an' ridin' a ragged edge,"
he remarked tolerantly. "There's one way to settle this and
make it final—"

"Name it, MacEwen!" Harve did not remove his eyes
from Pat's bleak face as he waited.

"There's five of us here." Brad was blunt. "We'll put
Stevens to the vote. If a majority says thumbs down, he
goes. Simple enough, ain't it?"

"I'll cast my vote for his stayin' right here—permanent,"
barked Harve instantly, with chilling significance.

"All right. And I'll give this cool hombre a break."
Doc spoke up with remarkable lack of heat. "I vote in his
favor, Wells!"

"I'll see you, Doc—and raise you one." Gila was stern.
"Against!"

Chet Denton found their veiled glances stealing in his
direction. With the vote of this drumhead court, no less
deadly for its impromptu nature, standing already two to
one against Stevens, the outlaw saw the full meaning of his
decision. To throw his weight in the scales with Wells and

Gila would be to damn Pat. Or with a bold endorsement he could even the vote once more. Instead of assuming a firm stand, Denton chose to offer instead what he considered a reasonable argument.

"Hang it, Harve—why be stubborn about this? Considerin' the stiff program yuh got laid out, we can use another good man and yuh know it—"

Wells cursed heartily, brushing over the appeal with venom. "Supportin' this Stevens, are yuh? That makes it two against two . . . MacEwen?" There was an evil warning in the glare he gave the young fellow, that dared any defiance.

Pat had been following these sharp exchanges with calm interest. Now he fastened his eyes curiously on MacEwen, showing no more than a polite concern for the outcome.

Considering that he was still in his early twenties, Brad himself exhibited admirable aplomb. Whether or not he gathered that his vote was inevitably for or against Wells, as well as Stevens, he did not hesitate.

"Stevens hasn't done a thing to me," he said casually. "Why should I say yes or no? But if it was up to me alone," he concluded, "he'd stay."

Doc began to chuckle harshly, evidently maliciously amused by the situation. "Well, that's three to two for Stevens, Harve—if I read these votes right. We aren't exactly against yuh, old boy. We just ain't with yuh." He could not help adding the unsubtle dig.

Wells glared around from face to face, his exasperation poorly concealed. He had not expected matters to go against him in this decisive fashion. "Supposin' it's a toss-up with you rattlebrained fools," he ground out, in a crafty attempt at persuasion. "I still don't savvy how MacEwen's say-so counts for so much. He ain't been with us himself for more than a matter of days—"

It was the first intimation Pat had received concerning Brad's actual status with this crowd, and to say that it interested him is putting it mildly. From first sight the young fellow had enlisted his thoughtful curiosity. Doc's apparent bias in Pat's favor could be largely discounted on the ground of malicious impulse; for whatever else he might prove to be, the man was obviously a hardened, cold-blooded criminal. MacEwen was another matter. Stevens had known him to be working about the Powder Valley range off and on for a year or more. To find him riding with owlhoots had been something of a surprise. Nothing could have demonstrated more clearly than Wells's cynical words that Brad was still an untried quantity.

"Well, that's true—" began Gila, scratching his matted and tousled head.

"But yuh took MacEwen in without a peep," Denton pointed out matter-of-factly. "How come you're so dead against this Stevens party?"

"I'll tell you that too." Harve was dogged. "Every extra man ridin' with us makes the cut just so much smaller, Chet. Have yuh thought of that angle?"

"Well, look here," MacEwen interrupted firmly. Once called into question, he was proving a stickler for detail. "You put on a front for bein' fair and square with us, Wells, by havin' Stevens here put to a vote. You got your answer to that, but no matter. How about this split Doc was askin' for? Do the boys rate a divvy—or wouldn't that be square?"

Stung by Doc's mocking chuckle, Harve would unmistakably have loved to crush this up-start then and there, and he would have done so but for his knowledge of this gang. He regarded Brad steadily through slitted eyes.

"Kind of mouthy, ain't you?" he grated thinly. "When I start takin' orders from you, punk, I'll let yuh know!"

"That's tellin' him off. On the other hand, Harve," drawled Doc with playful coolness, "I don't consider it a particularly good answer to the question—"

Wells did not pretend to show his rough side to Doc as readily as he had to young MacEwen. Scowling, he assumed his authoritative tone.

"Dammit, boys, this is no time to be thinkin' of liquor and cards. I'm carryin' the money—yes. Am I goin' anywheres? And what'll yuh be usin' it for? . . . What's the sweat, anyhow?" A new thought seemed to strike him, and one that flared his nostrils wide. "Ain't none of yuh figurin' on pullin' out, I hope—?"

"Naw." Gila spoke up for them all hastily, as if anxious to head off any potential difficulty. "It ain't that. But

you're so dang cagey, Harve! Yuh won't tell us nothin'.
Reckon we all like t' know what we're headin' into.''

"You'll be plenty busy, no fear.'' Wells paced back and
forth irritably. "All this blasted palaver is a waste of time.
We ought to be straddlin' leather right now—''

"Let's shove off then!'' urged Denton roughly. He was
starting for the horses when Harve halted him.

"Look, Denton. I've been tryin' to get certain things
straightened out before we start. You ain't been much
help.'' He swept them all with slow shrewdness. "Let me
put it this way . . . Just how much are yuh willin' to have
this Stevens know about us?''

They stared at him blankly. "Just what do yuh mean by
that?'' Gila demanded.

"Gila—boys—we none of us ever saw this hombre
before today.'' Wells had gathered his forces and was
driving the words home. "What do we owe him? We pried
him out of his jackpot, there on the range. He's in the
clear. Why can't he drift on his way, whatever that is, and
forget all about us?''

He was taking a different tone from his original frank
enmity. It was a concession, and Stevens by no means
missed the point. Anxious to be rid of him by whatever
means, Wells had a double purpose in pressing the question now.

Pat had followed with interest the outlaw's devious
attempts to steer away from any suggestion of parting
personally with the money they had stolen from Sam and
Ezra. There was satisfaction in knowing Wells still carried
it intact since it would be more easily recovered from him
than it would be if the loot was divided among the others.
For that reason alone, Pat was determined to stick close to
the gang until shifting circumstance made this no longer
possible.

"What's eatin' yuh, Harve?'' MacEwen asked incredulously. "There's five of us in this now! Kind of late in the
day to fret about one more—''

Wells raked the others with his glance. "Well?''

Apparently weary of argument, Doc shrugged an almost
indifferent answer to the leader's query. He glanced from
Wells to Pat with a half-smile.

"Mighty stubborn cusses, the both of yuh," he observed dryly. "Could be because yuh look somethin' alike, I suppose—"

"What's that?" Harve's words cracked sharply. His attempt to cover up his sudden alertness was a poor success.

"Sure," Gila assured him, as if trying to prevent a threatened clash. "Stevens does resemble yuh a mite, Harve. More than a little, I'd say. Hell, when I first seen him there in the brush I thought for a minute it was you—"

Wells stared in momentary surprise as he heard this. Although his eyes quickly veiled again, concealing whatever it was that had flashed swiftly through his crafty mind, he was not quick enough to hide the significance of the moment altogether.

"So you're all against me." Harve's grunt was stolid. "It don't mean that I hold anything personal against Stevens. I want yuh to understand that. I'll undertake to keep an eye on him . . . Meanwhile, I'll just ask yuh to remember that I tried to spell out a warnin'. Shall we head out?"

With the words, he appeared to be done with the subject of Stevens, and in fact, it was as graceful a backdown as could have been managed under the circumstances.

Taking to the saddle, Pat found time to wonder what it might spell for himself. If Harve Wells pretended to be reconciled to his presence, Pat was well aware it could only be because the outlaw leader counted on turning the fact of their resemblance to each other to his own advantage—a circumstance that promised trouble, if not outright treachery, for Stevens.

Dark had fallen over the range as they finished supper. While Pat knew the gang would travel safest at night on this range, it was plain even to him that Wells's purpose must be urgent indeed to drag him from the safety of the secluded gulch. Following the others only closely enough to insure against losing them in the gloom, he took particular care that none should come up on him unseen; a watchfulness which, for all the other's assurances, he extended particularly to the outlaw leader himself.

4.

THE NIGHT RIDE proved to last no longer than a couple of hours. Working out of the badlands, the outlaws rode up into the hills. A late moon, glowing obliquely across the rough slopes, told Pat they were crossing a corner of Rafe Alford's range.

Here and there they saw a few head of Rafter A stock bedded down in the sage. Doc and Gila looked them over, murmuring indistinguishably. But it did not take Pat long to guess what was in their minds. Enough steers were scattered about here to constitute a respectable haul; nor was there any semblance of a guard.

They passed on, however, crossing several wooded ridges. Far across the empty land Stevens finally glimpsed a twinkling light. Before many minutes he gathered that Wells was making directly toward it.

The rising moon revealed with increasing clearness the huge, spiny backbone and tawny slants of the Culebra range. Powder Valley yawned almost in its shadow, a vast misty gulf. Identifying landmarks with care, Pat nodded to himself. "That light has got to be Ernie Grapes's little Circle G spread," he reflected.

Grapes was a grizzled, silent, dour-visaged old-timer who had been living quietly here in the hills for several years. Since he claimed little rangeland, and that an isolated portion, cattlemen seldom mentioned him. His herd was in fact so small in number that he did all his own work, with the occasional aid of a growing daughter. It was impossible to guess beforehand what interest Harve Wells was able to find in any such modest set-up.

The men rode boldly down to the Circle G yard, making no attempt at concealment. The ranch cabin, a neat log affair backed by gnarled bullpines, nestled under the frowning bulge of a lofty granite cliff crowned with crags and topped by weathered spires. In this setting the house was little more than a faintly looming gray shape, marked by the beam of lamplight from one half-curtained window.

Wells crowded his pony forward to bang on the slab door. After some delay sounds could be heard from inside, and the scrape of a bar being taken down. The door opened on a crack. A grumpy voice called through.

"Yeh. Who is it?"

"Open up, Ernie." Harve gave his order humorously. "Yuh got visitors."

Pat waited, intensely curious to learn the outcome. A moment later the door swung wide and Grapes himself appeared in the opening. A lean man, broad and bony, but by no means decrepit, he held a smoking glass oil lamp aloft as his sharp eyes inspected the gathered horsemen.

"Harve Wells, ain't it? . . . And Doc an' Gila." There was wariness in his gruff tone, rather than welcome. He did not appear to recognize the others in the group. "What yuh after, boys?"

"We've come to see yuh, of course." Wells was as ingratiating as he ever became. "Limber up, Grapes! Yuh ought to scare up coffee for us anyhow. Don't be an old crab all your life—"

There was cajolery here which largely failed of its intended effect. Grapes continued to eye them all with unrelenting disapproval. "I dunno—" he began dubiously.

At that moment a young girl appeared at his side, calmly relieving him of the lamp, and glancing out with a complete absence of his own uneasiness.

"Nonsense," she smiled. "Tell them to come in, Dad. Mr. Wells, isn't it?"

Pat knew at once that this could only be Letty Grapes. She was perhaps nineteen, robust and pretty, with luxuriant black hair that just now flowed unconfined down her straight back. She had matured considerably since the one time Pat had laid eyes on her, several years back, on the occasion of her mother's funeral in Dutch Springs, while Letty was still a long-legged stripling. Her snapping dark eyes swept the outlaws with casual alertness; and he could have been mistaken in seeming to notice that her glance lingered briefly on young MacEwen.

Grasping the girl's indirect invitation hastily, Wells waited for no further urging. "Light down, boys." He stepped from the saddle and stepped swiftly toward the cabin, the others following.

Letty was already at the stove when they crowded inside. Stepping aside stiffly to admit them, old Ernie appeared to find no ready alternative but to make them grudgingly welcome. But he was not talkative, answering Doc and Gila's greetings with a grunt.

A rumble of masculine talk filled the place as some of them found seats. Pat stood back, taking it all in shrewdly. He could not help asking himself under what circumstances Ernie Grapes had known Wells and his companions in the past. That they were well and warily acquainted was unmistakable; and that fact alone seemed to carry its own meaning.

Letty made good coffee, strong and fragrant, which Harve and one or two others laced with liquor that Grapes had unwillingly broken out. Brad MacEwen did not enter into the general talk, drifting as if by accident toward the girl. Letty seemed neither to encourage nor repel him, exhibiting a thoroughly natural pleasantness. But more than once Pat caught a wistful expression flitting across the young fellow's face as he watched her.

"Well, Letty! How's my cowgirl been?" Wells broke in on their murmured talk with rough joviality.

"Pretty good, Mr. Wells." Meeting Harve's sally with distant respect, Letty accorded him adequate attention and nothing more.

Harve persisted in his heavy-handed way, appearing somewhat anxious to exclude MacEwen from the conversation. Letty deftly fended him off without seeming to do so; and Pat observed that she drew an obscure gratification from the expression of disgust gathering on young MacEwen's lean face.

The three-cornered exchange was of brief duration, largely unnoticed by the others; but it told Stevens much.

"Hanged if Harve Wells isn't smitten with this girl," he discovered to his amazement. "From the looks of things,

Harve is convinced she's bound to feel the same way about him. How could she resist the handsome brute?''

It went far to explain the attraction of the modest Circle G for the outlaw leader; and it might likewise reveal the true reason for Ernie Grapes's frank antagonism. Naturally the latter would not take kindly to the idea of this man shining up to his daughter. But for some reason Pat was not altogether satisfied that the matter ended there. More than a minor affair of courting was surely afoot here. Obvious undercurrents rendered the situation mysterious indeed.

One was the fact, gradually dawning on Pat, that despite the casual manner of both Letty and young MacEwen, they had clearly known each other for some time. It was revealed in the occasional glances which passed between them which told more than words could express. Neither was prepared to admit how much the other meant in terms of vital attraction; yet the truth crept through.

"I hope Wells don't catch onto this," mused Pat soberly. "But he's a thick-skinned hombre. Probably confident he can hold his own against such competition as Brad."

Distracted presently by the men's talk, Stevens turned his attention to Wells and their dour host. It did not take him long to determine that more than deep distrust lay between the pair. An atmosphere of deadly duelling lay in their brief and wary exchanges.

"Headin' down-country for the cold weather?" Grapes forced himself to address the renegade casually.

Harve's look was bland. "Not right off, anyhow." He seemed not to understand the oldtimer's query.

"I would, if I was you." Ernie sounded blunt. "Heard about Rafe Alford gettin' robbed," he proceeded doggedly. "An' there's a U. S. marshal around, too. Understand he's combin' the hills—"

Harve's slitted lids flickered. "That so? . . . He won't be showin' up here though. Might be a good idea for us to stay put for a day or so."

Ernie's expression was iron. He shook his grizzled head stubbornly. "I wouldn't, Harve."

Stillness fell. Wells glanced furtively about the faces of

his gang. "How's that, Ernie? A feller'd think yuh didn't want us around," he jested heavily.

Pat had gathered moments ago that both Grapes and his daughter understood thoroughly the true character of these men. Remarks had been passed that had been more revealing than any flat statement. As an honest rancher, the old man was hardly to be condemned for the position he took now.

"I don't, Wells. I want yuh to leave now—tonight. Yuh know that. An' don't bother me no more, neither!"

If it had come to an open clash at last, Harve accepted the reality with remarkable coolness. "Pah." He brushed defiance aside. "Cool off, man. Don't tell me an old hardcase like you scares so easy! We're stayin' as long as we want—in fact, I would now, even if I intended to move on."

He eyed Grapes almost smugly, as if daring him to do something about it. Ernie rumbled deep in his chest, glowering his helplessness. No one else said anything, MacEwen unconsciously moving closer beside Letty, who managed to conceal whatever surprise or resentment she might have felt.

"Sorry yuh feel this way, Grapes," Doc broke the tension in his oily way. "Reckon we all figured we could depend on yuh to that extent, after—" He paused significantly.

Ernie flushed, his lined mahogany face darkening. It was plain from his heckling response that he entertained fewer scruples against arguing with the bearded outlaw, and they tossed a few tart remarks back and forth. When Wells coldly put in a word, chill and final, Grapes gave up. Disdaining any further concern, he gruffly ordered Letty to her room and a few minutes later stamped off to his own bed, abandoning the outlaws to their own devices.

Totally unmoved, either by old Ernie's friendship or his enmity, Doc humorously moved that they bunk in the barn; and the others half-attentively agreed. Actually, from the moment of Grapes's disappearance, they appeared intent on some secretive subject, putting their heads together in a murmured conference to which Pat prudently paid no attention.

When they at last moved outside, Pat followed young

MacEwen to the barn. They were briefly occupied in finding satisfactory bedding in the hay, but it was only a short time before Pat observed that the others did not intend to follow their example at once. He remarked as much.

"No—they got business on their minds," returned Brad shortly.

Pat's ears pricked up. "What would that be?"

It was a moment before MacEwen responded. "It's those Rafter A steers of Alford's," he grunted then. "Wouldn't take three or four men long to gather a considerable bunch—and Gila got the bright idea of runnin' them over the New Mexico line and alterin' the brand to Tomahawk. It could be done easy with a runnin'-iron."

"I see." Pat began to conceive a more accurate notion of the true ambitions of this hard-bitten crowd. "Looks like they've decided they won't need you and me along—"

"They don't see any reason for cuttin' you in." Brad was plain-spoken. "As for me, I'm supposed to be keepin' a weather eye on Grapes!"

Pat read more than one shade of contempt and disfavor into the remark. It occurred to him that this was a good time to cultivate the young fellow who had interested him from the start.

"Wells seems to be roddin' a mighty tough crew, MacEwen," he observed conversationally. "How come you happened to drift into this racket?"

"Got to live, ain't I?" Conscious then of unusual curtness, Brad softened his tone somewhat. "To be frank, though, Stevens, I don't know. Chet Denton staked me when I was out of a job, and hungry. He hinted at work, and one thing led to another. Yuh know how these things will happen to a driftin' cow-prod."

It was logical enough. Yet Pat sensed that he was holding something back.

"Maybe you discourage too easy. Letty's a nice girl—and I expect old Ernie could use a good hand."

"Unh-uh." Brad chose to ignore his full meaning. "Grapes only runs a handful of stock. He couldn't afford even a part-time hand."

"But you ought to be able to remedy that," suggested Pat.

MacEwen demurred however. He seemed to realize dimly the girl's bent in his favor, and was not altogether successful in concealing his own hearty reciprocation of the feeling. But he was not prepared to do anything about it.

They talked desultorily before dozing off. Stevens learned enough to satisfy himself that MacEwen was not yet a hardened renegade; and as it turned out, proof came quickly the following morning, when he awoke at daylight to hear the distant lowing of cattle.

Wells, Gila and the other outlaws were sprawled about in the hay. They had stolen in sometime at a late hour. Weary as they must have been, they slept lightly and were awake once more at the first stirring.

"No trouble, I take it?" MacEwen remarked casually to Doc, as they sat up to pull on their boots.

"None that we couldn't take care of, at any rate," was the drawling reply.

"If there's any trouble at all, Mac," Harve Wells thrust in purposefully, "it'll turn out to be yours. You're drivin' that stock over the line to Harbor Canyon. Better climb up on your hindlegs an' get about it. Chet'll show yuh the way."

"Tryin' me out, eh?" Brad murmured colorlessly.

"Yeh." Wells came right back at him flatly. "We're tryin' yuh out, MacEwen. Is that okay?"

The young fellow shrugged, turning away to start down the ladder into the lower part of the barn. Ernie Grapes came storming out of the log house just as they reached the open. He was dark with rage and exasperation.

"Blast it all, Wells!" he roared furiously. "What're yuh up to now?" He jerked a violent hand toward the generous herd of Rafter A steers grazing openly in the valley below. "Yuh got your gall, drivin' that stolen stock plumb into my dooryard! Tryin' your damnedest t' drag me back into your crooked capers, ain't yuh?"

"What do yuh mean?" demanded Wells menacingly.

"I mean that yuh done this deliberate—tryin' t' bring the law down on my head! . . . You brought them steers here. I want 'em moved, an' moved fast—and you can pull your freight along with 'em, the passel of yuh!''

To Pat's surprise, Doc was the one who coolly took up the challenge, laughing quietly. "Easy, Ern," he advised dryly. "Ain't altogether forgot your old callin', I hope. Or didn't anyone ever ask where yuh got the money to buy this spread?''

Grapes was very near to apoplexy, glaring through a red haze of hatred. "I ain't forgot how to handle a hog-leg—if that's what you're drivin' at!'' He threw off Letty's restraining hand, as the girl sought vainly to calm him. "Come on. Get about it, now! An' fast—''

Like falling tumblers the facts were slipping into place as Stevens listened. He knew now what Ernie Grapes's mysterious past concealed. A one-time outlaw in his own right, and probably a formidable one, at some time Grapes had given the terrible game up—presumably with success until this crisis struck. Always, it seemed, an outlaw's friends became more deadly in the end than his most inveterate foes. It was so now.

Harve Wells's crude plan was equally clear. From the moment of their arrival here, the pressure had been unremitting, and old Ernie thoroughly understood as much. By dragging the grizzled veteran back into his crooked activities, not only did Wells stand to gain a wise and trustworthy ally, but it must also inevitably place Letty well within his reach.

Harve's bland face showed that he already had the old rawhide tight in his vise. But he knew better than to crowd Ernie too far.

"Slack off on the whip, Grapes," he urged pettishly. "The boys're startin' pronto." He transferred his colorless stare to MacEwen and Denton. "You heard Ernie, boys. Get goin'!''

Without a word the pair got up horses and set off. Little time was required in bunching the rustled steers, and ten minutes later the herd set off toward the south, whence devious mountain trails offered a promise of unobstructed passage to the territorial border.

His indignation unabated, Ernie Grapes stamped about, watching narrowly till the cattle were gone from sight. He waited in vain for Harve and the others to pull away, and at last made his way to the house in search of breakfast. To his disgust, nothing had been done in that direction. Nor was Letty anywhere in evidence, barge about and call as he would.

Doc and Gila had followed Grapes to the house, and it was only a matter of minutes before the answer dawned on them. Wells joined them there. He got it too.

"No use callin' the girl, Grapes," he taunted. "She's gone to help the boys drive them steers. Ain't yuh tumbled yet?" His pause was deliberate. "Come on in with us, old boy, or lose your daughter." The ultimatum rang out with cruel force. "It's plain Letty takes right after her old man. She's a natural, Ernie—and we'll make her better!"

5.

THERE WAS A MARKED change in the atmosphere of the Circle G following the recent developments. The owlhoots took charge as coolly as if having already won their point with old Ernie, although Pat shrewdly guessed the decision was only being put off.

"Come on, Doc—get in there and slap a breakfast together," Gila tossed at the bearded man. "I done the cookin' for this outfit yesterday. Danged if I'm doin' it all."

Doc waited only long enough to catch Harve Wells's nod of agreement, and turned resignedly toward the kitchen. A strangely docile man in some respects, he was no little surprised when Pat followed him.

"Don't tell me you don't trust my cookin'," he began, somewhat nettled.

Pat smiled. "Nobody likes to cook, Doc," he rejoined easily. "But I've filled in at roundup, in a pinch. I'll help you."

Apparently mollified, Doc fell to, and with Pat's aid soon had a meal ready to which even Grapes did justice. Doc glanced across the table at Wells as they downed the last of their coffee.

"Ain't this the day we're meetin' Hank?" he asked pointedly.

Harve looked startled for a moment. "By grab, I hope not! . . . Friday, ain't it?" He glanced around, fastening his glance on Gila.

The big outlaw shrugged. "Thought it was Saturday—"

"It's Friday, Wells," Pat cut in decisively.

They argued briefly before Harve turned at last to Grapes for a final word. "What day is it, Ernie? We seem to be all mixed up—but you keep regular hours,'' he concluded half-contemptuously.

Grapes looked dour, seriously inclined to refuse to help them. But at last he allowed a grunt to escape his folded lips. ''Reckon it's Friday, as Stevens says.''

Harve nodded, not at all out of humor. ''We're meetin' Detch Monday night,'' he announced. ''That'll give Chet and the kid till tomorrow to get back. We'll shove off as soon as they show.''

There was more talk, and putting two and two together, Pat understood that another, and this time carefully planned, job was in the offing. If Grapes drew the same conclusion from what he could not help hearing, he gave no sign that it meant anything to him.

Ernie made no attempt to ride off about his work this morning. He understood well enough that he was being watched; and although the outlaws sat around pretending to load, Pat presently realized that they were deliberately working on the rancher's cold nerve.

Sizable sums of money were carelessly mentioned which they confidently expected to divide after the robbery. Doc jestingly remarked that Letty would probably want to ride with them once she learned of the project. It must have been a goading torture to Grapes, who only clamped his jaws and looked away as he listened.

They kept at him quietly and persistently throughout the day. From the old rawhide's ominous manner Pat began to hope that, driven to desperation, he was secretly planning to steal away at the first opportunity and ride for the law. Once apprised of what was going on, Gif Towner would put a speedy end to this brand of persecution. But Wells and his two iron-nerved confederates afforded Grapes no more opportunity to slip off than they offered Pat himself.

An oppressive air of tension gradually closed in on the little ranch as the afternoon waned. Grapes began to stare off toward the south, though there was little enough hope of his daughter's return before morning. His fretful uneasiness during her absence was undisguised.

''That's young folks for yuh, Ernie,'' Wells remarked callously, reading his mind. ''Always dashin' around—lookin' for excitement. If yuh'd come in with us like a sensible man, I might be lookin' after Letty myself right this minute.''

Grapes said nothing, his slitted eyes like opaque agate.

Pat fried steaks for supper, and the evening dragged out in heavy silence. Harve Wells appeared obscurely relieved when dark fell. All day he had been under pressure of expecting the U. S. marshal's momentary arrival, and it was still possible. The doors were barred as a precaution against surprise and all lights shielded. None of them left the house tonight. Harve himself slept on a couch in the dining room, gun in hand.

They were awakened by a thunderous banging on the door at dawn. The outlaws were instantly alert, their rifles ready as they glided toward the curtained windows. But it proved to be only Letty and Denton and Brad MacEwen returning hours ahead of their time.

Wells sprang to tear the bar down and fling the door wide. He appeared extremely pleased to greet Letty.

"Hang it, girl! Yuh had the old boy worried," he exclaimed, showing both severity and indulgence in his tone. "I tried to tell him yuh could take care of yourself." Yet he peered suspiciously at Chet and Brad as if unable altogether to curb doubt.

"Everything's fine. We rode most of the night to get here," returned the girl hastily. "I think we were too busy for things to have a chance to go wrong—"

She was flushed, and somehow unnaturally cool. From her searching glance Pat saw that her chief concern was for her father. Ernie returned her look frowningly.

"You're all right, Dad—?"

"Yes—an' hungry," growled Grapes significantly.

Relieved, Letty began to laugh as she headed for the kitchen. "Hold your horses, crosspatch," she threw over her shoulder. "I'm dirty as I can be. I'll wash up and get busy in a jiffy!"

Breakfast might have been a cheerful affair but for Harve Wells's insistent probing. Wolfing his food, he hurled queries at Chet and MacEwen alternately, drinking the answers in.

"You made Harbor Canyon, I take it?" he snapped at Brad.

"Sure. Made it an hour after sundown. Turned the stock over to a man named Beneker—"

Harve glanced for corroboration toward Denton, who nodded.

"See anybody on the way here this mornin'? Anybody at all?" He shot the question this time at Chet.

Denton shook his head, looking interested. "Why? Somebody around?"

"Only a federal marshal," grunted Wells pointedly. "Have to get your rest the best yuh can, you two. We're headin' out of here today—"

"Where to?" It was MacEwen who asked.

"Buffalo Creek."

The men appeared to understand this. But Letty, serving young Brad with griddle-cakes at the moment, glanced at his impassive face quickly.

"I suppose that means another—job." She apparently failed to note the thunderous scowl on her father's face.

Harve began to laugh heavily, but it was Doc who spoke quickly in reply. "It sure does, girl. A long ride, and a little brisk action at the end of it. But you wouldn't be interested—"

She looked about uncertainly at them all, and Pat later observed her glance stealing toward MacEwen and settling there. Brad looked stubborn, although trying to pass it off lightly.

No more was said of what lay before them as the meal was cleared away. The men scattered to get up horses, scanning their surroundings sharply as they reached the open. One or two were busy assembling packs. Ten minutes later Pat accidentally came upon Letty and Harve Wells, hastily conferring outside the kitchen door. Unseen, Stevens drew back to cover, to listen and watch.

"You'll let me go along, won't you—Harve?" he caught the girl's low, urgent appeal.

"Why, I don't know now." Harve pretended tremendous doubt. "Why should *you* want to ride with a bunch of roughnecks like us, Letty?"

"Well—" Letty could not bring herself to add to this dubious explanation. But it was plain to Pat that Wells's fathomless vanity supplied the answer he most wanted to hear. Clearly Harve thought himself to be the real attraction, and just as plainly the thought gave him no twinge of regret.

"Go your own gait," he told her finally. "But it's up to you how yuh aim to get around your old man. He'll say no. And I won't say yes—to him. Unless," he concluded ponderingly, "he decides to go along too."

The girl could offer no honest encouragement on this score, and Pat turned away at that point, hearing footsteps near at hand. He went after his own pony. The gang gathered before the log house a few minutes later, ready to ride.

"Better come with us, Ernie," suggested Wells flatly.

Standing in the door, his face closed, Grapes shook a dour negative. On the moment, Doc began to chuckle icily. They glanced around in surprise to note Letty riding up from the corrals on a fresh bronc. The sight shook old Ernie.

"Letty!" he roared. "Slide off that horse an' get in the house!"

Not trusting herself to speech, the girl only shook her head resolutely. Doc's chilling laugh swelled louder.

"Better change your mind, hadn't yuh?" he taunted Grapes. "It can turn out to get awful lonely, here all alone—"

With burning eyes, Grapes watched as they turned to jog away. Obviously pleased, Wells drew close to the straight-backed girl and thereafter rode at her side.

Pat did not neglect to keep an eye on young MacEwen as they struck east, wondering how he would take this. Brad could not help glancing in Harve and Letty's direction from time to time. But he contented himself with observation, seeming to avoid their company rather than court it. Pat asked himself if it occurred to MacEwen that she was riding with the outlaws largely on his account. If it did, it only made him more secretive than ever.

They struck the plains before midday and made good time during the afternoon. If Marshal Towner was still in Powder Valley he did not appear. Long before dusk they were miles to the east. Occasional cattle herds appeared as they crossed the boundless plains, and from the cottonwood-choked hollow in which they pitched camp for the night, the Rockies rose in a jagged silhouette far behind them against the sunset sky.

Letty made a joke of preparing a camp meal for the band over an open fire which Wells zealously kept burning for her. Brad MacEwen was remarkably silent tonight, looking at no one; moreover, he kept back in the shadows. But it was Stevens's guess that he missed nothing.

Later Letty retired to her blankets in a brush lean-to, and the outlaws smoked about the dying fire. Little was said beyond a muttered reproof which Doc leveled at Wells. "Lot o' sense, bringin' her along." He jerked his head toward the girl's shelter, his tone sarcastic.

"Think so?" Harve was brazen. "Maybe I want her along for reasons of my own—"

"Good ones? For you, or for us?" inserted Gila cynically.

"Never mind. Wait an' see." Harve would say nothing further on the subject.

They had, in point of fact, not long to wait. Only a few minutes later Chet Denton half-rose from a rock to peer into the gloom. "Somebody comin'—" he muttered tensely.

As one man they melted away from the dim blaze into obscuring shadows. Almost at once Pat caught a faint thud and click of hoofs, and a moment afterward a mounted figure rode slowly up to the fire, reined in and stared gloomily about. "Anybody here?" he rumbled dourly.

It was Ernie Grapes.

Wells moved forward at once. "Well, well! Light down, Ernie," he exclaimed heartily. "Glad to see yuh decided to come along!"

The others showed themselves, nodding to Grapes and saying little. Still Ernie sat rocklike, turning his head as he probed the darkness. "Where's my girl, Wells?"

"She's all right," Harve assured him quickly. "Probably asleep already." He pointed out the shadowy lean-to.

Grapes got down heavily, and it was MacEwen who took charge of his horse. Grapes had come to stay, however hard he found the decision. There was some low-voiced talk, but finding himself pointedly excluded, Pat presently turned in. The others followed his example before long.

Rising early, they shoved on in the gray of the morning. Ernie Grapes might have long been one of them, he fitted so smoothly into this crowd. The others appeared to understand that, whatever his reasons might be, he had elected to throw in with them unreservedly; and, for a wonder, all Doc's jibing and Gila's cynical incredulity disappeared.

They shoved on briskly across the bunchgrass plains. Good spirits prevailed, with the possible exception of old Ernie. He was frankly laboring all morning under a heavy burden, and when they pulled up for a brief halt at noon he flatly declared himself.

"Look here, Harve," he spoke up abruptly. "I'm ridin' with yuh—under one condition."

"What's that, Ern?" Wells looked concerned.

"That girl goes back. This ain't no place for her, an' you know it!"

Harve's face said that he had not anticipated this. "Well, I dunno." Scratching his head, he turned toward Letty. "What about this, Letty?"

She had unmistakably avoided her father during the morning, and now looked innocent. "What about what?" she countered.

Harve grew flustered. "Ern here wants yuh to go back home—"

"I heard him." Letty was remarkably unruffled.

"Are yuh goin'?" Wells found the question hard to get out.

The answer came with a snap. "No."

There was some brief bickering, both Gila and Doc putting in a word. But Letty stuck to her guns. Harve shrugged, glancing smugly at Grapes. "If you can't manage her, what can I do?" he seemed to be saying, secretly more sure than ever that his charm for the girl was proving irresistible.

Grapes retired gloomily into himself, saying no more. He made no attempt to turn back. Done eating, they shoved on. They were in no hurry now. Pat guessed they had not far to go, and this proved the case. In late afternoon they reached a hidden camp deep in the brush alongside a meandering creek which Gila called the Buffalo. Here they drew up.

Undercurrents ran through the entire gathering as the evening dragged on, with little to do now but wait. Grapes brooded, while Letty tossed her head. Harve Wells appeared elated, and Gila and Doc scowled at the girl in perplexity. Brad MacEwen watched it all alertly.

Nearly all of them seemed primed for an explosion; but all this was speedily forgotten the following morning, in fresh breezy sunlight, when Denton, standing guard, rode in early with another man, sallow and furtive of face, whom Wells hailed as Hank Detch.

Detch was the messenger and spy they had awaited. A conference was called at once, and the gang got down to business. Pat learned with a jar that a train holdup was planned for that night, at Sedona on the Denver & St. Louis mainline. Wells plotted the job in minute detail, assigning a task to each man. Ernie Grapes himself was to take part in the actual stick-up, and he did not demur. Pat alone was not included, which caused him to suppress a smile.

A hitch in the carefully laid plans occurred at the last minute, however. Sedona was ten miles away; and making ready to start in midafternoon, the men went after their horses. Pat saw Ernie's mount suddenly begin to rear and buck. MacEwen offered to bust it, but Grapes was grim. Hauling in the bridle reins hand over hand, he managed somehow to crawl astride. Then the pony, a wall-eyed bay, abruptly unwound. Men yelled, scattering out of the way, and Grapes sailed through the air to land in a heap. Harve Wells ran to him.

"My God, man! That was a nasty toss. Are yuh okay?"

Ernie took his time looking himself over. "Skinned my leg a little—" But when he tried to rise, the leg crumpled and he went down, to sit panting and white-faced.

Wells cursed luridly. "Dammit all! Yuh done that crazy stunt a-purpose!" he charged, furious.

Pat abruptly understood that Grapes was out of the stick-up for good as a result of his mishap. "Easy, Harve. I'm prepared to go in his place—if yuh want me," he offered coolly before Grapes could reply.

Harve shot him a black look. Hesitating briefly, he shrugged his brawny shoulders. "We'll see—"

Doc was looking around for Letty. "She can stay here an' take care of her Pa," he proposed gruffly. But the girl was nowhere to be found, having jogged away a moment before with MacEwen. Harve turned decisively to Pat.

"You're the goat, Stevens." He smiled darkly. "I figure you'll stay with Ernie and like it!"

Secretly relieved, Pat watched them ride away. It took some minutes to get Grapes moved into camp and settled comfortably. He chuckled bleakly then.

"Tough luck for us both, Grapes," he remarked. "I sure thought this was my chance to make a fast buck—"

Eyeing him attentively as he winced with pain, Ernie proved himself no fool in a dozen words. "Don't be too sure yuh won't turn out to 've been there anyhow," he growled.

It sobered Pat. "You mean—my resemblance to Wells?"

"You'll get your answer," Grapes shot back dryly. "All in good time, boy!"

6.

IN FULL FLIGHT, with slugs buzzing about their heads, Ezra and Sam Sloan placed several miles between themselves and the aroused outlaws before they ventured to haul up and take stock of the situation. Both were mortally provoked with Pat Stevens. They knew now why there had been no discussion of the expected meeting with Harve Wells's gang. Pat had known from the start how he intended to ingratiate himself with that bunch, and he had accomplished it smoothly, with complete success.

"He's a cute one," groused Sam. "Probably managed t' get himself in solid with Wells, just as he figured. But he sure left us out in the cold." He turned a sad eye to his lanky partner.

Ezra shrugged. He was of the same opinion; but if Sam thought he meant to give up altogether on that account, he was much mistaken.

"One o' them hombres follered us quite a ways," Ez muttered. "Wonder if we finally managed t' shake him off—"

Sloan gazed back watchfully and long. No sign of pursuit was to be seen, but Sam was obviously thinking hard. "If we could reach Gif Towner again in a hurry," he hazarded, "we could make it hot for them birds!"

Ezra was not impressed by this reasoning. "Where do yuh reckon Towner'll be now?" he growled.

Sam got the point. "What'll we do, then?"

"Them buzzards chased us, didn't they?" Ezra spoke flatly. "We'll chase 'em right back!"

"Well—" Sam sounded dubious. "We can trail 'em, o' course. If yuh can show me where it'll do any good."

Ez showed his impatience. "Stevens is with 'em, ain't

44

he? He may need help when he gets ready to make his play. Could be he'll need it bad—an' I aim t' be there.''

It silenced Sam. Taking a roundabout course, they turned back in the direction from which they had come. Because of the nature of the range it was impossible to cover ground with any rapidity while concealing their advance, and the afternoon sun was low by the time they once more approached the point at which Stevens had left them so unceremoniously.

While it was almost certain the outlaws had ridden on, they dared leave nothing to chance. Ezra worked down through the pine growth where Wells and his men had taken cover. It did not take them many minutes to discover that the owlhoots had indeed gone away swiftly.

Ez picked up their sign without any trouble. It was not difficult to determine that Stevens had gone on with the outlaws. But now the partners were forced to proceed more warily than ever. For the trail of the gang was a winding one, abounding in patches of cover where ambush was possible at every turn. Working it out without haste, Ezra looked up suddenly in disgust.

"Danged if it ain't gettin' dark already," he muttered. "Thought for a minute my eyesight was goin' back on me!"

Ten minutes later, so swiftly does night fall in the mountain altitudes, they were forced to stop. If they meant to stay with the tracks, they could do nothing more till morning.

"What now?" Sam inquired.

They had a few meager supplies with them, packed from Stevens's Lazy Mare ranch. Ezra was in favor of putting up where they were, and his squat companion did not argue the matter.

Riding off the trail a hundred yards into a dense stand of balsam, they hauled up for the night. There was some low-voiced discussion of Pat's luck with the outlaws, but silence soon fell as they wrapped themselves in their blankets.

Chilly dawn found them finishing a patched-together breakfast, and by the time it was light enough to see, Ezra was bending over the trail once more. Nodding to himself, he clambered into the saddle and they thrust on.

The going grew rougher as they proceeded. The trail became rocky, retaining little impress of the passage of horsemen. Before a full hour had slipped by, Ezra glanced ahead with a frown. "Hell," he growled. "We're runnin' plumb into a patch o' badlands——" A thought struck him as he gazed, and he halted Sloan abruptly. "Hold on, Sam. There ain't more'n a dozen or twenty acres o' that broken stuff altogether—an' yuh might as well try t' track a bird over them rocks as follow a trail."

Sam was clearly disgusted that their night's wait had led to no more than this. "So it ain't a very big patch," he snarled shortly. "So why don't we ride right on through it——?"

"Don't yuh get it, stupid?" Ez was scornful. "Them busted gulches're a made-to-order hideout! Ten to one Wells himself is in there somewheres right this minute——"

Sam tightened up in a flash. "What in tunket are we doin' here, then?" he whipped out. "If they've posted a lookout, he's spotted us aready!"

Hastily retiring to safe cover, they mulled the subject, discussing it tersely. If the outlaws were cached somewhere in this jumble of rocks, it would be possible to smoke them out without too much trouble. But to do so would have been like tackling a hornet's nest. Both understood, moreover, that it was not their present object to betray their own presence. Sam once more broached the idea of locating the federal marshal. But Ez scoffed at this.

"These birds move fast. They could be in Texas by the time we find Towner an' get him out here," he pointed out.

They finally hit on the scheme of watching the badlands from a vantage point, enabling them to follow the gang once the latter were seen leaving. After some study Ezra selected a tall butte overlooking the area, and leaving their horses picketed in the rocks, they crawled to its crown.

As they hoped, the butte afforded a fine view of the surrounding range. But the broken, eroded badlands yielded none of its secrets to their prying eyes. Lying flat on their bellies, they watched for a long time, hoping the smoke from a campfire might betray the outlaws' position. Sam finally grunted with exasperation. "This could turn into a long grind," he muttered discontentedly.

Ez was short with him. "If yuh can suggest anything better, we'll do that," he rasped.

The down-beating sun grew hotter as the morning dragged out. They began to suffer from thirst, and Sam clambered down for the canteen on one of the saddles. Noon came and passed, and they had seen nothing.

"Dang it, Ez," Sam burst out at last. "I don't believe them birds're down there at all! We ain't seen smoke, nor a horse or guard or nothin' else!"

Ezra seemed inclined to argue. But he could not deny the logic of Sloan's reasoning. Even the most cautious band of outlaws might have been expected to betray their presence in some manner.

"So what'll it be?" the lanky redhead grumbled sourly.

"Dunno about you—but I'm goin' down there an' make sure." Sam sounded determined. "I'd just as soon risk flyin' lead as lay here an' get a sunburnt behind!"

Proceeding afoot, after descending the butte they worked slowly and carefully down into the maze of barrancas and gulches. So extensive did the rocky maze prove that the afternoon was waning once more by the time they found their way at last to Wells's hidden camp in the gulch. It was empty and silent, although they made out clearly enough that the owlhoots had recently visited the place.

"Shucks." Sam gazed about the rocky walls with a vacant expression. "This is one time we was left holdin' the bag."

Retrieving their horses, they now did what they should have done earlier, circling the broken area in the hope of picking up the trail where it emerged from the gulch. But the ground was so rocky that evening once more caught them at a loss.

Again they camped where they were, although Sloan had begun to lose hope. "Ernie Grapes's little spread can't be more'n a few miles from here. Whyn't we ride over tonight," he proposed, "an' ask if he's seen anything?"

Neither was to know what might have occurred had they acted on this casual suggestion. Ezra canvassed the pro-

posal briefly and brushed it aside. "Can't trust these crochety
old-timers," he mused. "Grapes might think we was nosin'
into *his* business."

Sam allowed the proposal to drop without protest. They
spent the following morning in fruitless search for the lost
trail, and the afternoon was no more successful. On the
third night they gave up, their supplies having finally run
out. The following day was spent at the Bar ES, where
they caught up on their ranch chores. Sloan rode north to
the Lazy Mare next morning, to learn whether anything
had been heard from Stevens. Crusty Hodge could tell him
nothing, and for the moment they seemed to have come to
a dead end.

But anger at their inexplicable failure would not allow
Ezra to rest. Bright and early on Tuesday he proposed that
they should ride into Dutch Springs, where at least they
might keep an ear to the ground, and after the usual
heckling objections, Sam agreed.

Jogging into town, they were turning in at the hitchrack
below the Gold Eagle Cafe when a man in the act of
mounting his horse made them wait briefly. The big man
swung astride, and as he turned to glance at them recognition was mutual. It was Marshal Towner.

"You two, hey?" The lawman's eyes slitted under the
shaggy brows. "Maybe yuh wouldn't mind explainin' what
you're doin' here—"

Reminded thus of their bad luck, Ezra felt under no
compulsion to be civil. "If we was where we wanted t' be,
we wouldn't be here," was his brief retort.

Towner's seriousness said that he had no intention of
overlooking this kind of talk. "A little more of that, Ezra,
and I'll take you into custody." His tone sharpened.
"You've got your nerve, showin' up here as it is."

Sam eyed him levelly. "Slack off, Towner, till yuh hear
our story," he advised soberly.

While he related briefly the ruse by which Pat had
succeeded in joining Wells's gang, leaving him and Ezra
behind, Towner listened shrewdly. As he went on to outline their own movements, it came to Sam that the lawman
was not putting much stock in the tale. He broke off.

"Dang it, man! Don't tell me yuh think I'm lyin' about this—"

It proved to be the wrong approach. The marshal never took his eyes off them as he replied. "Maybe it's news to yuh that the D & SL night express was held up last night at Sedona, and your friend Stevens was recognized," he said evenly, as if quite sure they knew all about it. "Nothin' was said of you two—but I suppose yuh could've been overlooked!"

They stared at him. "Sedona? . . . Why, that's seventy miles east o' here," rumbled Ezra. "Just how fast do yuh reckon we are, Towner? An' yuh know yourself that if Pat can be mistook for Harve Wells, it could happen the other way around too!"

"Quick on the trigger, ain't yuh?" Towner was not to be easily swayed. "Yuh come up with an alibi, quick as a flash!" Keen and growing suspicion made him breathe audibly. "Yuh *could* be right about yourselves," he conceded gruffly, after a pause. "But I won't buy that about your smooth pal. Too smooth!" Obviously convinced that he had been hoodwinked, he was enraged.

"Alibi, huh!" Ezra snorted. "Go ahead an' punch holes in it, then, Towner!"

"I will." Gif was grim. "Won't take me long to get about it, neither!"

"In that case we'll be goin' with yuh," Sam rejoined promptly. "If yuh come up with somethin' on Stevens, Marshal, Ez an' me aim to know all about it."

Towner delayed an instant. But his case against the pair was after all weak; and it occurred to him that their presence would afford him an unparalleled opportunity to keep an eye on them.

Without further delay they headed down-country. Reaching Hopewell Junction before noon, Towner pulled strings and a boxcar and light engine was placed at their disposal. Two hours later they were on the D & SL mainline, speeding east, and a run of another hour found them pulling into Sedona.

Gif conferred briefly at the station with railroad detectives, and they were presently ready to start. As near as was known, the bandits had boarded the night train in

Sedona, run it down the track a few miles, and fled north after the robbery. Towner set out, west once more along the right-of-way, with Sam and Ezra in tow.

There was no doubt about the point where the robbery had occurred. One of the gang had been waiting with horses, and the ground was scuffed up considerably. The lawman was still nosing around the tracks when Ezra picked up the trail leading away. "Come on, Towner!" he exclaimed. "This is a cold trail, an' it won't get no hotter here!"

Towner jogged after them, studying the ground. Noting the tracks which led north, he grunted. "You're a tracker, old man," he allowed tersely. "Whatever else yuh are!"

Ez slanted a burning glance at Sam and shrugged expressively. They shoved on, following the trail as fast as Gif was willing to move. It was midafternoon when they picked up the outlaws' sign, and they were still following it through desolate and lonely range country when the afternoon began to close in.

Nor were they in better case when falling dusk forced them to pull up. "Now yuh know how we fared, tryin' t' track them hombres," Sam told Towner.

Gif scratched his grizzled head. "Does seem like we're in the middle of nowhere, for a fact—"

"No such thing." Ez was terse. "There's a cowtown eight or ten mile north o' here. Antler, or some such place."

"That's so." Towner glanced about. "Do yuh think Wells was hittin' for Antler, Ezra?"

"Don't think nothin'." The redhead was not to be tricked into proposing a course of action. But the marshal was capable of making up his own mind.

"In a pinch, we can come back here in the mornin' and take up where we left off," he pondered.

Sam saw what he was leading up to and was ready to go. "Let's go." He started his horse. "At least we can grab a bite in Antler. An' there's no harm in lookin' around."

Darkness fell, and their progress was necessarily slow. Toward nine o'clock Ezra spotted a flickering fire in a wash. Towner ordered the pair back, and proceeded with utmost care. They drew up at length on the night camp, and leaving the horses, stole through the brush on foot. A single elderly man sat brooding over the fire, and he scarcely bothered to glance up as the U.S. marshal strode forward.

Close behind Towner, Sloan took one look at the lined and somber face, and grunted. "Danged if it ain't Ernie Grapes," he exclaimed. "What in time yuh doin' way out here, Ernie?"

Grapes looked them over without the flicker of an eye-lash, and if his face looked gray it may have been the effect of the firelight. "Been workin' roundup on the Z-Bar-A," he vouchsafed grudgingly. "Skinned my leg an' it looks like I'm laid up for a day or two—"

"Z-Bar-A, yuh say?" Ezra was puzzled. "Never heard of it—"

Grapes did not bother to reply. Towner looked around. "This is no cow-camp," he murmured. He and the seated man exchanged stony glances.

"No—I got hurt over here aways. Bronc throwed me. The boys wanted t' move me, but I said no," Ernie felt impelled to explain in some detail.

It struck Sam as strange that the Powder Valley rancher should be found this far from home, although Grapes's tiny spread could hardly pay well, and he might easily enough have wanted to pick up a few dollars. Whatever the answer, it was no part of Sam's intention to voice random suspicions of his own in the hearing of the hard-faced lawman. Towner nosed about a few minutes longer and, without further comment, prepared to push on. Once more in the saddle, he paused to look around.

"See any strangers around here?" he asked flatly.

"No." Grapes did not so much as look up.

Gif clearly had something on his mind as they rode away but whatever it was he kept it to himself. They reached Antler an hour later. The town was fair-sized, considering its isolation. They stoked up at a lunch counter and made the rounds of the local bars without finding anyone known to them. Towner only shrugged, and it was at his suggestion that they turned the horses into a livery barn and crawled into the hay.

Awakening late in the morning, they breakfasted and went for their horses. Little was said, and they were standing in the street, ready to start, when Sam suddenly dropped his reins with an exclamation.

"Hey—!" he whipped out suddenly. "Ain't that Stevens himself standin' over there?"

He hastened across the street and waddled hurriedly up to a man who, talking to several other men, certainly did resemble Stevens considerably from the back. Sam's bristly jaw thrust out. "Well," he exclaimed gutturally. "Give an account of yourself, yuh old horsethief—"

He had hardly got the words out when the man whirled sharply. His rising elbow caught Sloan flush in the eye, knocking him backward. Sam tripped and sat down. He had never been more surprised in his life than he was by what happened next. Mingled alarm and rage in his soul, he scrambled up in time to see the man he had been so sure was Pat hurrying toward an alley near at hand. Not once did he glance back. An instant more and he was gone.

7.

IN THE CAMP on Buffalo Creek, on the night of the train robbery, Pat had a lively sense of what must be going on while he waited. Grapes felt it too, stiffening at every faint sound from the brush. It was plain from his manner that he bitterly regretted his position. Pat was satisfied that Harve Wells's cajoling had had absolutely no effect on the old rawhide. He was here solely on Letty's account, and for no other reason.

Ernie's dour silence, moreover, proved that he thought he had made a mistake in immobilizing himself. Unable even to guess to what risks the girl was being subjected, he was equally powerless to protect her. But Grapes was stoic. Fending off Stevens's attempts to talk with an occasional growl, he finally put an end to them by rolling up in his blanket.

Although Pat was faintly astonished, he could not help admiring the man. He sat by the small fire, thinking hard. There was nothing now to prevent him from riding away to carry a warning of the outlaw's plans to some sheriff. But it was already too late actually to prevent the robbery; and there would be infinitely more advantage to Marshal Towner in learning where the outlaws rode afterward. Nor was Pat likely to forget the money belonging to Ezra and Sam.

It was that which caused him, after a long wait, to move close to Grapes and listen attentively. Incredibly enough, the man was asleep. Moving quietly, Pat made a methodical search of the meager packs that had been left lying about camp. Finding an old jacket belonging to Wells, he examined it thoroughly, without result. Harve's slicker yielded no more. Forced to give up finally, Pat realized the outlaw leader's suspicion of his fellows was such that he was probably carrying on his person the stolen Bar ES horse money.

After replenishing the dying fire, Stevens sat down to wait. When the outlaws returned they would be coming fast, and he had no expectation of rest for himself. Yet it was deep into the small hours, and he had dozed off more than once, when a crashing in the brush not far off jerked him broad awake.

He had time to shake old Ernie roughly by the shoulder before Gila burst into the faint firelight. He came alone, hauling his lathered bronc down with an iron hand.

"Come on, Stevens! Ready t' pull out of here, or ain't yuh?" he barked. "What in hell yuh been doin', anyhow?"

Without a word Grapes was getting himself ready to travel as speedily as possible. Pat soon had the horses saddled and ready. Gila rolled a pack or two together with careless haste, and scattered the fire with a single kick of his boot.

"Where's the bunch?" Pat demanded, hoisting the disabled Grapes into the saddle.

"They ain't lost," Gila answered tersely. "Get goin', man!"

Pat swung astride on the fly, and they stampeded off through the darkness at the outlaw's heels. A thin sickle moon barely showed them the way. As they climbed a shadowy ridge a mile farther on, the mournful hoot of an owl caused Gila to swing to the right. A few minutes later they joined the restlessly waiting group of dark figures under a cottonwood clump.

"All right, boys. Let's drift—"

It was Wells's rasping voice. Ernie Grapes's prompt response was like the crack of a whip. "Hold on, you . . . Where's my Letty?"

"Right here, Dad." The girl's tone was tight. "Please—we must ride on at once!"

Ernie's grunt was scarcely one of relief. "Well, I'm as ready as I'll ever be."

Sweeping out from under the trees, the horses thundered north in a close group. For an hour they maintained the same driving pace, with only an occasional barked direc-

tion or admonition from Wells. Gradually the tension grip-
ping these men began to relax.

Not yet had any sign of pursuit materialized to the rear.
But they well knew this was not their most imminent
danger. Word of the bold train holdup would spread rapidly, and it was not improbable that the law might be lying
in wait in almost any quarter.

A faint streak of coming daylight was just cracking the
gloomy eastern horizon when Pat saw Harve Wells crowd
his pony toward Grapes as if he had something on his
mind. He peered into Ernie's face intently.

"How's that game leg?" he demanded. "Givin' yuh
any trouble?"

"Keepin' up, ain't I?" Grapes retorted shortly.

Harve did not let up on him. "I want to be sure yuh'll
go on doin' it, old man."

Ernie disdained to respond to the surly challenge. Wells
stuck at his side for some moments longer as if wanting to
say more. But he was conscious of Letty hovering near;
and not since the unceremonious start from the camp in the
brush had Pat drifted more than a few yards away from
where Grapes rode. Harve seemed to give over at last and
reined away.

They hauled up at full daylight in a brush-cluttered
hollow and made scalding coffee. It was gulped down with
relish. The men moved about, stretching their cramped
legs and watching the back trail narrowly. But Pat knew
that Wells intended to cover many hard miles before this
day was ended.

Letty hung about her father with frank concern. Ernie
was irritably inclined to rebuff her. More than once Brad
MacEwen approached the pair, only to steer away again.
Perhaps he concluded to let well enough alone for the time
being. Doc was the most serene member of the bunch, and
it was soon clear that his amiable remarks were intended to
ease the general tension.

"Shucks, Ernie, there wasn't no trouble at all. Slack
away, can't yuh?" he told Grapes cajolingly. "Letty wasn't
within a mile of flyin' lead. Nothin' dangerous about
holdin' a bunch of horses—"

Ernie's bushy brows cocked fiercely. "Yuh mean she

led the broncs right up t' that train?'' he rumbled menacingly.

Doc laughed at him. ''Well, that's where they was
needed most,'' he pointed out coolly. ''Yuh can see for
yourself that we put 'em to good use!''

Grapes folded his lips sternly, slanting a look of contempt toward Wells, but saying no more. Hurt by his
curtness, Letty turned away dejectedly. It was the opportunity young MacEwen was looking for, and he joined her at
once. Harve and the others were gravely discussing their
future course at the moment, and only Pat was close
enough, pretending to work at a loose cinch-strap, to catch
a word or two. He cautiously watched the two over the
back of his horse.

''Letty, this is your chance to get Ernie home—before
somethin' bad happens to him,'' the young fellow urged,
strong appeal in his tone.

''Why, he'll be all right,'' rejoined Letty hurriedly.
''I'm only worried about his ability to stay with us. After
all, *he* hasn't done anything yet that could be held against
him.''

There seemed a concealed barb in the words directed at
MacEwen himself, and Pat's ears pricked up. For some
time he had been doubtful of just what to make of this girl.
A moment later he was sure.

''Well, it's you *I'm* worried about—if you want it plain,''
Brad muttered, flushing. ''This rotten deal is no place for
a girl, Letty. You must see that.''

Her eyes widened in well-simulated surprise. ''Me!'' To
Pat's ears at least, her light laugh was artificial. ''Why,
Brad! Put your mind at rest, if that's all that's bothering
you. I may as well admit I'm having a perfectly swell
time—''

''With Wells hangin' around you every minute, breathin'
down your neck?''

She gazed up at him with wonderful self-possession. ''But
I've hardly noticed that! It is hardly any concern of yours,
anyway. I tell you I'm having a fine time, Brad . . .
Aren't you?''

This time there was no mistaking the knife. Letty was
trying her best to awaken him to his true position. Pat

sucked his breath in. He had experienced in the past the
subtlety of women—and despite her fresh, tanned, open
face and dancing eyes, this girl was a woman grown.

"If this isn't the damnedest setup I ever barged into,"
Stevens reflected with amazement. "Old Ernie's got himself tangled up with this gang on Letty's account—and
she's here because she's worried about MacEwen. Brad
won't give her a tumble, for some reason; and meanwhile
Wells is makin' his own play for the girl." His brows
wrinkled uneasily. "Maybe it's a good thing Harve doesn't
even guess he'll never get anywheres."

The smug authority that was nourished by his own
inflated ego made Harve appear certainly the most confident of them all. He turned now to call out in his gruff,
heedless manner, "Okay, now—hit the leather."

Swinging astride, they lost little time in following as the
leader struck boldly out across the rolling swells of empty
rangeland. Once more the pace was unrelenting. Although
genuinely hurt, Ernie Grapes hung on stubbornly. Wells
glanced sharply in the other's direction from time to time,
but he soon found that it wouldn't be necessary to prod the
tough old-timer.

Noon came, and their halt was briefer than before.
Whatever Wells's objective, he drove toward it with hard
intent. From an occasional remark passed, Pat gathered
that this was unfamiliar country to most of them. But
Grapes showed that he had long and unerring acquaintance
with the plains when he finally voiced a loud protest.

"Blast it all, Wells!" he jerked out as the afternoon
lengthened. "Yuh must know what you're doin'. *I* say
we're takin' a mighty foolish chance."

On occasion Harve was capable of assuming a curiously
conciliating attitude toward the other man. It was so now.
"So what's bitin' yuh, Ernie?" he inquired plaintively.

"Yuh know blame well we ain't ten miles from Antler!
An' that's too close!"

Wells regarded him with a hard smile. He took time
deliberately to glance about their surroundings, nodding to
himself at what he found.

"This is as good a place as any to set yuh up in camp,
Grapes," he dropped levelly as he dismounted. "I know

how far we are from Antler—and we ain't a bit too
close . . . Tomorrow mornin' early"—he detonated his bomb
casually—"we hit the Antler bank. I figure we stand to
pick up a pretty pot of money in short order." He broke
off with a bland and guileless look. "Yuh probably won't
be in shape yet t' join—us?"

Grapes ignored the question, slid to the ground with a
groan and glared at Wells with colossal disgust.

"The Antler bank, eh? So that's it!" he shrilled hotly. "I
didn't think yuh could be such a fool, Harve Wells!"

Not at all put out, Harve shook his head smilingly. One
of the characteristics hard to understand about him was
that he seldom did the expected thing. "That's where
you're wrong," he denied good humoredly. "Nobody'll
be lookin' for anything of the kind—so soon, anyhow.
We'll make our strike an' get away easy!"

Listening alertly, the outlaws were content to follow this
rattling exchange without comment, at least until they had
it all.

"But what in hell's the object?" Grapes fired out. "Yuh'll
keep it up, Wells, until yuh cut the ground clean out from
under us all! We'll never have a chance to get in the
clear!"

"Not at all." Harve was cool and hard. "My game is
all figured out, Ern, and it's mighty simple . . . I don't
aim to stay in this risky racket forever, runnin' and hidin'
for years—pullin' a job here and there just to eat, and
bein' laid by the heels in the end. Not me!"

"So—?" Grapes stared at him sharply.

"Why, we're runnin' up a string of quick jobs and
gettin' it over with," explained Harve smoothly. "No
better protection in the world than big money, when you're
tryin' to hide, and that's what I'm after. Once I'm well
heeled, I'll pull clean out of this country for good. By
keepin' our heads down and usin' common sense, we'll all
be safe," he concluded blandly.

That this outline included few or none besides himself,
except Letty, whom he undoubtedly planned to take with
him, no one except Pat appeared to notice. Gila, Doc and
Chet Denton seemed mainly struck with the shrewdness of
the leader's bold scheme; perhaps each had his private

notion of how much of the loot he meant in the end to claim. Not one demurred at the thought of the many dangers involved.

"What about this here bank, Harve?" Gila put in. "Know anything about it at all—or do we go it blind this time?"

"I've been in the place." Wells seemed to evade rather than meet the inquiry, for he went on at once: "This is how we'll work it, boys."

Prefacing his plan with the remark that they would split up and ride into Antler tonight for a look around, he proceeded to assign tasks and specific positions to the various members of the gang. He surprised some of them by announcing that MacEwen, Doc and himself were to pull the actual holdup, Gila and Denton covering them from strategic positions outside the building.

"Leavin' the girl outa this altogether, huh?" remarked Gila, with approval.

Harve's chuckle held a chill. "Not by a jugful," he retorted coolly. "Letty'll walk into that bank ahead of any of us. I want her to size the place up real careful. She can tip us the sign when we move in if we're makin' a mistake . . . Okay, Letty?" He turned his heavy smile on the girl.

"No sir! It ain't okay," Grapes cried promptly and harshly. "You're deliberately throwin' her into the worst possible danger! Keep it up, Wells, an' I'll be forced t' square accounts with you!"

This was a brand of talk which all too often led to trouble. Instant silence fell over them all.

"I'm against your scheme too, Harve," young MacEwen put in quickly, trying to fill the gap. "I'll grant yuh it's smart—up to a point. But don't forget lead may begin to fly in that place; and what's more, Letty won't be able to run when we take off . . . Yuh wouldn't want her to be left behind," he pointed out with some cunning.

"Don't worry about me, Brad MacEwen," Letty spoke up unexpectedly, with spirit. "I daresay I know how to take care of myself."

"But you simply don't know what you're gettin' into, girl!" protested Brad strongly.

"Don't I?" The look she gave him was veiled and not

altogether friendly. "You'll be there yourself. But I suppose that's different!"

Pat could not prevent himself from entering the argument at this point, although he knew Wells was prepared to listen to him with little patience.

"Leave the girl here with her dad," he advised the outlaw plainly. "I know you don't like the idea of cuttin' me in, Wells. But I'd rather run the risk of that bank for nothin', than let her face it. All the boys feel pretty much the same way, I expect—"

If Wells recognized his concern for Letty at all, he sneered it away. "Mighty big of yuh, Stevens. But it happens this time I've got your chore already cut out for yuh."

This startled Pat. "That so?" he said colorlessly. "What'll I be doin'?"

"Yuh'll be holdin' the horses ready, somewhere on the edge of town." Harve's remarkably flat tone was ominous. "There better not be any slips either—"

Stevens grunted. His face was wooden. "Worry about yourself, old boy."

Harve scanned him briefly, and nodded. "No worryin' will be necessary till it's too late," he remarked, turning toward the others. "Okay, boys. Get yourselves ready. We can leave what little grub there is with Grapes, here, and sneak a meal tonight in Antler."

There was brief activity while the horses were watered and guns looked over with care. Pat saw to it that old Ernie was made comfortable for the matter of hours he was to remain here, and Letty rewarded his thoughtfulness with a look of gratitude. Brad MacEwen likewise stuck close at hand—but for another reason, as it presently appeared.

Choosing a moment when the others were occupied, the young fellow turned to Pat, speaking hurriedly in a lowered voice. "I don't owe yuh much, Stevens, except good will—but keep your eyes peeled, there in town," he warned cryptically.

Aware in a flash that MacEwen suspected treachery, most likely at Harve Wells's hands, Pat put on a look of blank innocence. "We'll all be doin' that, I shouldn't wonder. Any special reason for mentionin' it, Mac—?"

Wells accosted them sharply before Brad had time to reply. "Get a move on, you two," he ordered roughly. "Time's in our favor now, and we ain't wastin' a second of it!"

Without a further glance for each other, the pair swung to the saddle. With Harve at their head, and Letty calmly falling in line despite her father's stern disapproval, the gang struck out in the direction of Antler.

8.

IT WAS TURNING DUSK when they sighted the outskirts of the plains town. In common with other supply points, Antler was surrounded by a loose scattering of weathered hay barns and sheds. At this hour it was possible to approach the place without being observed, and Harve Wells took full advantage of the fact. Staying away from used trails, he led the gang to the rear of a rambling, tumbledown shed which from its appearance had not been used for some time.

"We'll leave the broncs here," muttered the leader, glancing about with hawklike vigilance. "Yuh can all scatter into town from here—an' stay away from each other. Yuh'll see me around. If I give any of yuh the high sign, follow me to an alley or somewheres before yuh speak."

They indicated their comprehension, dismounting and preparing to depart. Doc gallantly offered to escort Letty, since her appearance alone in the streets might be apt to excite comment.

"Stevens, you've been elected horse-guard," Wells said levelly. "May as well start now. It's up to you to graze these broncs and keep 'em out of sight," he proceeded. "But we want 'em right here and damn handy, from daylight on tomorrow mornin'."

"All right, Wells." Pat saw that he was not intended to show his face in Antler, and probably might go hungry as well for all Harve cared.

The outlaw continued to hammer on what was expected of him, while some of the others drifted off. Brad MacEwen was not one of them. He lingered deliberately, and when Wells turned away, Brad moved toward Pat. Stevens saw the maneuver, and surmised the young fellow meant to renew his previous warning.

MacEwen got within two or three feet before he spoke. "Stevens—" he muttered guardedly.

Pat whirled away from him in pretended surprise at the harsh bark of Wells's voice, breaking in on them with instant suspicion.

"MacEwen!" Harve's tone was knifelike.

Brad shrugged. "Yeh?" he answered with evident disgust.

"Yuh was tryin' to say somethin' to Stevens on the sly, just then. That's the second time now—" he accused. "What was it?"

MacEwen wrinkled his nose scornfully. "What's the difference, Harve? Yuh wouldn't believe me if I told yuh—"

Wells looked daggers at him. "There's somethin' between you two!" he stated flatly.

"Sure there is!" Brad showed exasperation. "I want him to see that my pony gets an extra good feed of grass! . . . It's some gaunted, and I needn't tell yuh I'm goin' to need it in good shape."

Wells let the seconds go by, and finally jerked his head authoritatively in the direction of town. "All right. Shove along now."

Muttering to himself, MacEwen departed. Gila had waited for Wells, and after a few more curt instructions for Pat's benefit, the pair were the last to move off, fading from sight around the corner of the shed.

Left alone with the horses, Pat paused in the act of gathering the hanging reins. Not since joining this crowd had he deliberately left himself open to treacherous attack; but MacEwen's repeated attempt to put him on his guard seemed a clear sign of special danger. He racked his brain to guess what it meant. Perhaps Wells planned to take advantage of their mutual resemblance in some manner.

There appeared no certain answer, and Pat was about to give it up when a faint movement near the shed attracted his close attention. The place was sadly dilapidated, all its slab doors sagging where they were not gone altogether; and in the nearest, faint against the gloom of the interior, his sharp eye detected the crouching form of a man.

Even as Pat whirled that way he knew beyond doubt who it must be. It was Harve Wells, returning alone, the faint glow from the western sky gleaming palely on the sixgun in his hand.

Stevens had met too many sudden crises in the past to mistake this one. Dropping the gathered reins in an instant, he sprang away, diving for the thick brush in an oblique course away from the skulking outlaw's position.

Wells's gun cracked flatly in the evening quiet. Pat caught the droning whine of the slug. His stratagem had been successful, however, so that although the ball tugged sharply at his shirt, it made no more than a hot furrow across his ribs. Almost automatically, as he crashed awkwardly into the brush with a strangling cry, Pat's thoughts clicked into action. Instinctively he had drawn his own gun. He let it pitch ahead of him, to be lost in the mesquite tangle. And falling heavily, he gave a sighing groan and lay deathly still.

It was long minutes before anything whatever happened. Then Wells's stealthy footsteps slid close. He caught Harve's tense, harsh breathing, and stilled all movement as a match flared within feet of his back. After burning some seconds, it flickered out; but Wells was not satisfied. An exploratory hand sought Pat's holster, found it empty, then roughly rifled his pockets. Harve straightened with a grunt when his fingers encountered the blood-soaked shirt.

"That'll hold yuh, Stevens! Yuh'll stay put till you're found," he ground out with satisfaction.

There was a moment's pause, followed by cautious movement. Pat risked opening an eye and saw Wells separate a horse from the others and drive it into the brush. It was Pat's, and it would not drift far. Shortly thereafter Wells gathered the other horses and, mounting his own, led them away in a body.

Pat lay long after it seemed reasonably certain he was alone, pondering the meaning of this development. Harve had determined to dispose of him, but he was by no means satisfied that this was the bottom of the affair.

Rolling over finally, Pat made sure the coast was clear and rose. It was nearly full dark now. He used his neckerchief to stanch the bleeding under his ribs. Remembering his gun then, he got down on all fours and located the weapon, suffering a scratch or two in the process. It took longer to find his horse, and by the time he secured the bridle once more he found himself a safe distance from the ominous shed.

"Well!" he thought frowning. "Looks like time to lay my cards down with old Grapes."

No longer, certainly, could the hazards of staying with Wells's gang be ignored. Brad MacEwen was, Pat knew, the key to this tangled situation. But for him neither Letty nor old Ernie would have become involved. Not yet had Pat made up his mind about that young fellow. Was he bad at heart, an outlaw by natural inclination, or was there some other answer? Stevens had done his best to cultivate Brad without noticeable result. There still remained the hope that he might be able to move Ernie Grapes to belated action.

Pat's sense of direction had always been good. Despite darkness and unfamiliarity with this range, he turned away from Antler to strike out straight for the spot where the old rawhide had been left in camp. He was two-thirds of the way there, moving along at a good pace, when something caused him to haul in sharply. He slid his bronc into a wash and peered over its lip without making anything out in the gray gloom.

But patience was rewarded when, several minutes later, he heard the distinct thud of approaching hooves. Straining his sight, he made out the faint silhouette of several dark figures moving against the dim starlit sky. The men rode past without talking, and for some time afterward Stevens delayed to ponder. Who were they? Had members of the gang ridden back this way for some devious reason—or had the law already cracked down to carry Grapes off?

After following the wash only long enough to escape detection, Pat broke into the open and raced on. Urgency rode with him now. He knew how quickly disaster could strike at Letty through her father. Racing through the brush, he came more than once to where he was sure Grapes had been left. Not only was the land now empty and silent, but he could find no trace of the dead campfire he half-expected to come across. When ten minutes later a

gleam of light flickered across the dusky range, he sighed
with relief. In a matter of moments he was almost upon it,
noting the oddly motionless figure of Ernie seated before
the flames. He swung down while still on the run, and
broke into camp brusquely.

"Here we are, Grapes!" His tone was curt. "And it
looks as if Harve Wells was done with you and me."

Ernie gave him a keen glance. "Caught up with yuh, did
he, Stevens? . . . Well, I ain't done with *him* yet by a long
chalk!"

"Expect I savvy how you feel, old boy—" Pat broke
off short, his voice flattening. "Had visitors tonight, didn't
you?" He waited for the reply.

"Yeh." Grapes's voice was guttural. "It happens a
U. S. marshal stopped by. Seen him yourself, I suppose."
He was watching Pat closely.

"Deputies with him?" The query came like a shot.

Ernie drew his own inferences from this. "Couple," he
nodded. "A one-eyed, rough-lookin' hombre, an' a short,
fat—"

Pat waved a hand. "I know."

He suddenly knew a lot. He had let Gif Towner and his
friends pass unrecognized, within yards, not daring to
show himself. Perhaps even now it was not too late to
warn them of Harve Wells's impending plans. But as Pat's
mind worked on the problem, he relaxed somewhat.

"Like as not they were headin' for Antler, wouldn't you
say?" he queried.

"Didn't ask." Ernie's face was gloomy and set. "Worst
thing I could've done, Stevens—"

Pat nodded his comprehension. "It would only tip Towner
off, of course. And if the marshal's in Antler when Wells
pulls that job at the bank, he might grab Letty."

Grapes revealed by his agitated manner that Pat had
pointed up his own deepest fears. "Harve knowed the law
is on his tail!" he exclaimed doggedly. "Gif Towner ain't
the only one that's been waitin' for him t' overstep—"

"I don't intend to wait," rejoined Pat coolly. "Why do
you suppose I'm here, anyhow, Grapes?"

Ernie's narrow glance stole toward him, and away again.
"If I bothered t' ask myself," he muttered, "I'd say yuh

was maybe a spy. An' I reckon Wells knows somethin'—or he suspects!''

There was grim humor in Pat's nod. "He declines to take any unnecessary chances, at any rate. He tried to kill me tonight."

Some of the old fellow's stiffness had broken down. "Was he makin' a mistake, Stevens?" he asked bluntly.

"He made a great mistake not to finish it." Pat confronted the other squarely. "A few days ago, Grapes, Wells stole several thousand dollars from the two men you saw with Marshal Towner. And they happen to be good friends of mine. Does that answer your question?"

"More or less," assented the leathery rancher, almost cheerfully "Thought I'd seen yuh round Powder Valley. But—" He frowned. "MacEwen comes from there too, and yuh've seen what *he* is . . . Yuh ain't figurin t' turn me in, Stevens?" He waited, taut with alarm.

"I'm trying to save your neck, Grapes—along with Letty's, of course."

The old rawhide's face fell. "Aw, well. Dunno what luck yuh'll have there—"

Pat stared at him. "You don't?" He spoke sharply. "Then she's a better actor than I thought . . . Grapes, MacEwen is her reason for ridin' with this crowd. Her only reason, I'll be careful to add!"

"Brad MacEwen?" For a moment Grapes was struck dead silent. Then he exploded: "Thunderation!" He looked completely amazed. "I *thought* I seen her eyein' him. Then she give him the brush-off—an' I reckoned it was Wells. Damn his handsome mug!" He drew a deep breath. "Yuh almost give me hope, Stevens!"

"A woman will go through hell for the right man, Ernie," Pat told him dryly. "You should know."

Grapes's cheeks flushed scarlet. His wife had died, still pathetically faithful, while he was heedlessly riding the owlhoot trail. He had been shamed into the straight and narrow by the sorrow of her death—and the necessity to take care of Letty.

"What can the young fool be thinkin' of, then?" Thinking angrily about MacEwen, Ernie began to struggle to his feet. "Does he know, Stevens?"

"He probably guesses," replied Pat soberly. "Haven't had time or opportunity to talk to him myself—"

"*I'll* talk to him. Like a Dutch uncle!" Grapes burst out irately. He was in a rage seeing a young fellow making the same mistake he had made in careless youth. "Go get my horse, Stevens! We're ridin' for Antler."

The grizzled old badger seemed to be filled with new spirit. All his fatalistic hopelessness was gone. Pat thought this a decided improvement, but he also thought it wise to voice a warning.

"Whatever you do, Grapes, keep your head," he cautioned. "We may not be done with Wells—"

"Yuh mean you'll waste time speakin' to him again?" Ernie was incredulous.

"I'll polish his boots long enough to gain my point." Pat's simplicity was chilling. "He won't be sure how much I know. And guessing don't count in this game. When he finds my hand at his throat, he'll *know*—and it'll be too late!"

Pat got up the old-timer's horse and they methodically broke camp. It was after midnight when they set off; and jogging along at a moderate pace to accommodate Ernie's injury which was healing now but still stiff and sore, they found themselves approaching the supply town in first thin daylight.

They drew up at a willow-bordered creek not far from the edge of town. "Better stick here, Grapes, while I drift in for a look around," advised Pat. "It won't be easy to find folks at this hour."

"Get Letty, Stevens, an' drag her out o' there." Ernie was harsh.

"I'll certainly try. But it'll take time. If yuh hear fireworks," added Pat thinly, "take off. I'll do all that can be done."

Riding toward town alone, he weighed his chances. If he could locate Ezra and Sam, all would be well. There was equal possibility, however, of running into some member of the gang. Pat played his cards boldly, reaching a side street and striking into the main drag. His pony's hoofs echoed as he rode alone down through the business section. An early riser or two paid him no heed, and farther down the street a swamper was sweeping out an empty bar.

Racking the bronc, Pat turned into a livery barn to examine the stabled horses. He would be able to recognize the Bar ES roans he was looking for immediately. But he had no luck. A second try was no better. It was possible, of course, that Towner and the partners had not even stayed in Antler overnight.

Pat ate breakfast in a hash-house and was about to leave when he spotted Gila across the street. He quickly handed the cook a tip and slipped out the back way without being seen. But his operations would be hampered now. He tried unsuccessfully to reach the boardinghouse and turned away when he saw Doc idling on the porch. Pat's nerves began to tighten. Wells had the town posted—and time was passing. Already Antler's street was filling with men. All too soon it would be the hour for opening the bank.

Hurriedly exploring places where he thought Sam, Ezra and the marshal might be found, he was on the point of hunting up the local law enforcement officer when suddenly a rumpus upstreet attracted his attention. Men began shouting, waving their arms and running.

"Blast it, I'm too late!" Pat thought in disgust. "Wells has turned loose already—"

He whirled and ran for his racked pony. The thunder of gunfire ripped the morning quiet in the direction of the bank as he swung astride. He wheeled that way. He had barely got the animal in motion, raking the spurs deep, when the crowd in the street scattered sharply. Guns flamed as stampeding horses burst into the open. One raced this way, buck-jumping, half out of control as its rider swayed drunkenly.

All Pat's intentions were thrown abruptly out of gear as he recognized Brad MacEwen. The young fellow had been hit. There was blood on his jaw and a wild look in his eyes. In a twinkling Pat jumped his pony alongside.

"Keep goin', MacEwen! It's Stevens," he rifled. "I'll support you—"

Brad gasped and clutched at Pat's arm. They swept round a side-street corner and thundered toward the open range. Gradually MacEwen straightened up.

"Ain't bad hit! I was—stunned, Stevens!" he murmured. "I'll—make it now!"

Leaving Antler rapidly behind, they flashed toward the willow-lined creek and were soon there. Ernie Grapes was nowhere to be seen. But Pat did not pause.

"Did Wells name a gatherin' place, Brad?"

"Lava Rocks—a dozen miles north!"

Pat saw they were distancing a straggling pursuit now, and swung his mount north. "Come on, boy! We're ridin'."

9.

WHEN SAM SLOAN slowly got up, after mistaking a stranger for Pat Stevens and being knocked down for his pains, he swore heartily for a moment and finally turned away with a crestfallen air. His companions had witnessed his misadventure. Marshal Towner's lips twisted in a grim smile.

"What's the trouble, Sloan?" he said. "Don't your friends know yuh?"

Sam scowled. "Stevens wouldn't never have bunged me in the eye that way." He explored it tenderly. "That was some hombre I never seen before in my life—".

"Sure of that, are yuh?"

Sam stared his momentary surprise. "Certainly I am. Knowed it two seconds after I opened my mouth," he persisted stoutly. "Hang it, Towner, this ought t' be proof that some hombre lookin' like Stevens is sashayin' around!"

But Gif Towner only shook his head dourly. "If you're talkin' about what just happened, it could be proof that Stevens don't want any part of yuh, too. Seems to me he proved that by the way he took leave before."

"Yuh mean yuh think that *was* Stevens, just now?"

The answer was deliberate. "I'm not prepared to swear it wasn't—"

Sam snorted his exasperation, looking expressively at Ezra. "Yuh see how it is, Ez! Only way we can prove that gent wasn't Pat is to show Towner it was somebody else. An' to do that we got t' catch up with him—"

He was racking his bronc once more as he spoke, and without argument the other two followed his example. Sam was barely willing to wait for them.

"Come on," he growled urgently. "He ducked into that alley yonder." Already he was halfway to its mouth, beckoning them forward impatiently.

They strode through to a tangle of back yards littered with dismantled wagons, boxes and piles of lumber. No one was in sight at the moment except a clerk sweeping a cloud of dirt out the rear door of a market. But Sloan busily poked about for some minutes, assisted by Ezra and—with less enthusiasm—Gif Towner.

It was the latter who finally came to a halt with a grunt. "You're wastin' time, Sloan! Stevens didn't wait."

Ezra had been absorbing the lawman's persistent needling about Pat for some time without saying anything. But at this he whirled angrily on Gif.

"Dang it, Towner! Don't keep sayin' that," he roared. "Yuh go on actin' like *we* had t' prove the boy's no crook—an' that ain't the case. Right now Stevens is goin' out of his way to do yuh a favor! What do yuh want, blood?"

Towner was an officer of the old school. He had been in harness too long to exhibit any remaining faith in the good intentions of men. His only acquaintance with the notorious Harve Wells was through photographs, none of them too clear; and no one had bothered to deny Pat Stevens's remarkable resemblance to the owlhoot. Since his one and only meeting with Pat, Gif had found himself unable to forget that others had done most of the talking, and that he had foolishly allowed himself to be persuaded. If he suspected that allowing Stevens his freedom was a mistake, the train robbery which almost immediately followed seemed confirmation in full.

"I might as well say now that I don't trust him *or* you any further'n I could sling a bull by the tail," Towner retorted to the lanky redhead's angry challenge.

"Oh, hell." Sam made no effort to conceal his contempt. "Yuh said a minute ago we was wastin' our time. I'm inclined to believe it now—if this is the thanks we get!"

"It ain't your time I'm worryin' about." Gif was terse.

For some reason his meaning came across more ominously than before. Both froze, regarding him narrowly. It was Sam who spoke.

"What would that mean?" he asked with caution.

Towner let him have it. "It just struck me that yuh might be leadin' me around by the nose for this Stevens's benefit," he declared flatly.

"No such thing!" Sloan's face went black. "Why, you dang old—"

Before he could say more the crack of a gun rang out. It came from the direction of the street, and quickly falling silent, the three looked that way. For an instant there was dead silence. Then a sixgun slammed repeatedly, the shots spaced and vicious.

Towner was the first to wheel and start for the alley on the dead run.

"C'mon, squirt!" Ezra yelled over his shoulder at Sam. "Somethin's tore loose out there! It looks this time as if we'd tricked ourselves!"

Abandoning the fruitless search for the man they were sure was Wells, they broke for the street.

After dealing with Sloan in the street, Harve Wells slipped into the alley and threw a sweeping glance backward. He made out Ezra—and the burly lawman standing nearby was not unknown to him.

It was matter for some faint surprise to Wells that Marshal Towner should be in Antler. But this did not disturb him in the least. If the stark truth were known, it fitted in precisely with the outlaw's secret design, provided no hitch occurred.

Harve's intricate plans for the attack on the bank were clicking smoothly. Even now it was only a matter of minutes before the time set to strike. He had just nicely time enough to disappear from sight in the street, circle a couple of buildings, and saunter into the bank on the heels of Doc and MacEwen five minutes after the doors were opened. It suited Wells's sardonic humor to be coolly engaged in looting the institution at the same time that Gif Towner and his companions would probably be running through alleys and back yards on a wild goose chase.

Darting expertly across the back of a store, Wells pushed into the rear of a saloon, stepped nonchalantly out the front door and proceeded directly to the front of the bank. Doc and young Brad had paused in the door, one handing the other a match. Harve glanced around, to spot Gila lounging directly opposite. Denton pretended to be doing something with their horses, racked in a row a couple of doors down. He was not missing anything.

Letty was not in sight, and Wells took it for granted that she had already entered the bank. He looked meaningfully at the two in the doorway, and they turned and stepped in, with Harve at their heels. They paused just inside, backs to the door and covering him, as Wells took an instant to click the lock on the inside.

Then, unnoticed, he pushed past them and scanned the place sharply. The lobby, which was far from ornate, resembled a range country post-office with several teller's wickets and a door or two leading to inner offices. There was a window in front and one opening on a side alley.

Nearly a dozen people were in the place this morning, three or four men talking together in a group at one side, the others queued up at the only open wicket. It could not be helped, and Wells had taken it into account. He saw Letty standing at the end of the line as if waiting, and the girl turned at the same moment, looking at him with wide eyes.

Harve's raised brows asked a swift question. Strangely enough the girl did not respond directly, although she moved aside nervously, the action taking her near the talking men.

Wells took the byplay to be in the nature of a warning. He did not delay. The others saw his Colts flash out, and they followed suit.

"All right, boys—over against the wall."

It was said conversationally. Yet the words obviously struck an icy chill through every townsman present. Doc herded back the line at the wicket, his steely gaze giving warning.

There was a flurry of movement among the talkers as one of them shoved roughly away from the others and attempted to pull a gun. Letty started back with an exclamation as the outlaw leader's gunbarrel swung that way. She bumped the hard-breathing, elderly man behind her and his Colt clattered to the floor.

"Stand aside, sister!"

Wells surveyed the luckless citizen from under level brows. His eye caught a glint on the man's vest. "Local sheriff, eh?" He started to chuckle, only to stop himself sharply. One hand swept up to twitch his neckerchief across the lower half of his face with lightning swiftness.

It might have seemed a useless gesture, belated as it was, to anyone unacquainted with the outlaw's cunning mind. He had already been seen, as he knew; and this suited his intentions, although it was not in his game for others to suspect as much. He gave the local lawman and his companions a hard stare.

"Watch these hombres, you." Harve tossed the words at Brad. Next moment he sprang to the wicket. "You two at the desks! Stand up an' turn your backs—"

The clerks inside did as instructed, and for the time being the situation appeared to be well under control. Harve turned from the wicket and, lifting a foot, gave the light door leading into the cage a powerful kick. The lock snapped, and as the door shuddered open Harve sidled through.

"Okay—you with the pretty vest." He was glowering coldly at the youngest of the clerks, holding out a gunny sack which he had been carrying folded under his arm. "Be a good lad now, an' fill this with bills—yuh can start with them gold certificates," he added, nodding toward a stack of yellow-backs on the counter.

The clerk hastened to comply, his movements awkward. A taut silence held the uneasy group in the lobby, broken only by a nervous throat-clearing which brought a growl from Doc. Wells glanced back swiftly.

"How is it out there?" he rapped.

"Shut up an' get busy!" Doc snarled back. Smooth as he might be when he chose, he was all business now.

For all his apparent haste, the clerk seemed to be having trouble gathering a sufficient bulk of bills to please Wells.

"In the vault with yuh, an' load that sack on the double!" Harve demanded, prodding him with a gun. The clerk's mouth flew open; he started to speak, and checked himself.

"Get!"

Harve was jabbing the young clerk again with his gun-muzzle for emphasis, when a thunderous banging on the outer door echoed through the place. Brad MacEwen whirled toward the cage, his face bloodless.

"Shake it up in there! Time's runnin' out—"

Harve took a gliding step toward the stalling clerk, his

jaw set like iron. With an involuntary groan, the other jumped to the heavy vault door. It had barely started to swing wider when suddenly a sixgun crashed from inside the vault, smoke belching out into the cage. Harve was not hit, but his rage knew no bounds. He realized what must have happened. The president of the bank had been caught at work inside the vault when the holdup started, and had prudently laid low. But there was a revolver in the vault, and when he knew the clerk's enforced entrance must betray his presence, he had cut loose.

Stepping gingerly aside, Wells blasted several shots into the steel vault, hoping they would at least bounce around on the metal. He did succeed in silencing the man inside; but the roar from the shots was a complete give-away to whoever was banging on the outer door.

A slug screamed through the front door panels. MacEwen leaped aside and Doc crouched. They still dared not altogether ignore the men they held at gunpoint, and it struck the young fellow forcibly that their situation was tight and was becoming rapidly worse.

"Come on!" MacEwen rifled sharply. "We're gettin' out of this!"

Wells must have leaped to the same decision in a flash. He had sand, but he always preferred to bet on a sure thing. With a snarl he snatched the poorly laden sack from the teller's grasp and tossed it over his shoulder.

"This way, boys!"

Harve had spotted a door leading into the rear part of the building, and he did not intend to face the open street. Something could have happened to Gila and Chet Denton, and he had no wish to join them in misfortune.

Brad backed into the cage door, his guns still covering the lobby. But Doc proved more intrepid, or more stubborn. Walking coolly to the front window, he glanced out. He saw nothing of Gila or Denton, who should have been guarding the street. Instead, a grim-faced blacksmith spotted him from across the street and deliberately leveled a carbine.

Doc turned away, scowling, as the window crashed into fragments about his feet. He waved MacEwen on through. His glance swept the men in the lobby, barely touching

Letty, who had backed into a corner. Before passing into the cage, Doc swung his gun sidewise and casually shot out the glass of the side window opening on the alley.

Wells already had the rear door open. Doc thrust Brad ahead of him. "Snap it up!" he ordered. "They'll have that alley covered. They may watch it long enough for us to slip out the back—"

The door Harve had discovered led into a dismantled and dust-covered lumber room containing only a collection of wooden boxes, stacked papers, and filing cabinets. In the rear wall a couple of dirty, barred windows gave limited glimpses of the open yard. Detecting hazy movement out there, Wells paused.

"Try this," Doc snapped, indicating a barred and sealed door apparently leading into the adjoining building, which they knew to be a hardware establishment.

Harve did not hesitate. Loud, scuffling sounds of movement could already be heard in the bank. Men cried out, their words muffled. Tearing the bar down, Wells jammed his brawny shoulder against the door. It groaned without yielding. Harve and MacEwen hit it together on the second try and it sprang open with a bang.

They ran through, to find themselves in a kind of storage shed stacked with nail kegs and other supplies. No one was about, but across the shed a sliding door stood ajar, revealing the worn planks of a loading platform. They made for it. Wells yanked the bandana off his face and sheathed his guns. The gunny sack was tucked casually under his arm once more. With him in the lead, the trio stepped out into the side street.

"Swell." Young Brad's tone was wire-drawn. "We made it, anyway. The broncs're just around the corner here—"

No one was in sight as they moved that way, sternly curbing all signs of haste. Not till they had nearly reached the corner were they accosted—and then a man ran up behind them, his boots slapping the dust sharply.

"Hey!" he burst out. "They're robbin' the—"

Before he could say more, MacEwen's gun swiveled and crashed. The man's hat sailed off. With a ludicrous expression of amazement he sprang for cover.

"Yuh dammed fool!" Wells hurled at Brad. "What did yuh do that for?"

Doc pushed them furiously toward the horses. "Get aboard and dig!" he blared. "In two seconds they'll be on our necks!"

He was right. Men grouped or crouching along the street whirled to face their way. Guns broke into a chattering uproar. The horses reared, stamping. MacEwen was the first astride. He started away. Doc swung up lithely to follow him, but Wells succeeded in heading the latter off.

"Other way!" Harve yelled. "You'll never get through there! They've got Brad already!"

Doc saw MacEwen weaving unsteadily in his saddle, his bronc plunging wildly down the street. He swore, but Wells still blocked his path. An instant later they wheeled the ponies and struck the spurs in. Slugs buzzed about them as they whirled into an open lot and disappeared from sight; and though Doc kept looking back for MacEwen he could not make out what had happened to him.

But if Brad's wild shot there in the side-street had seemed willfully to bring discovery and pursuit down on them, it was by no means wholly without design. MacEwen alone had bothered to remember Letty, abandoned alone in the bank to face the outraged local sheriff.

As the rattle of gunfire broke out, the men in the bank rushed into the street, led by the disgruntled lawman. In the excitement of the moment, there was no one to observe the girl slipping quietly out behind them and moving rapidly away. She knew it might be only a matter of minutes before they remembered. Reaching her horse, thoughtfully tethered some distance apart, she turned its head and rode directly away from the scene of the excitement. A few minutes later found her passing the borders of Antler and striking out alone, her heart beating loudly as she glanced cautiously backward. So far she was not followed. Letty struck her spurs in and rode off into the enveloping brush.

10.

LAVA ROCKS was a dark, eroded jumble of pinnacles and caves said to have been a favorite haunt of the fierce Cheyennes in earlier days. Situated on the crest of a sweeping rise, they could be seen, standing gloomy and desolate, for miles around. Since the rocks had the further advantage of being surrounded by hard flinty ground, it was next to impossible to track a horse that way.

Harve Wells had been on the spot before and recognized its potentialities. He therefore had not hesitated to name the rocks as rendezvous for the gang following the whirlwind bank holdup.

Harve and Doc were the first to arrive, less than an hour after their unceremonious departure from Antler. Leaving the horses in a natural amphitheater providing perfect cover, the pair climbed to a high ledge that gave a wide perspective of the rolling plain beyond. Little had been said as they made good their escape, but from their faces it was plain that both were thinking hard.

"Things didn't go off—ah—exactly as you planned, there in town," Doc said in mild criticism, combing his spade beard with thoughtful fingers.

Wells was disgusted. "Nowhere near as big a haul as I expected," he assented gloomily. "Somethin' went wrong outside the place, or we'd had a lot more time—"

"Yeh." Doc managed to sound remarkably dry. "Makes me wonder if we'll be seein' Gila or Denton again!"

Soberly they discussed the fate of the pair, but reached no sure solution. "Could be they spotted somebody in the street, and pulled their freight in a hurry," offered Harve at length.

"Who would it be?" countered Doc briskly. "We had

the local badge-toter right there in the lobby! Hell, it was Gila's business to head off trouble, not run from it!''

Wells shrugged off the mystery. He had no intention of mentioning the federal marshal, so there was no other explanation to offer. ''Maybe now yuh'll admit that that girl's okay.'' He thus changed the subject abruptly. ''She did herself proud there in the bank! Even made it look innocent when she bumped the sheriff's arm.'' He looked faintly bothered. ''I warned her to have a good story ready if they questioned her . . . If she shows up in the next hour or so, we better move on—''

''Yeh.'' Doc was regarding him steadily. ''You—an' me—an' that dame. Shook the bunch down pretty hard, didn't yuh, Harve?''

Wells flushed. ''They could all still show up,'' he defended gruffly. ''Nobody belongs in this business that can't look after himself!''

''Yuh got an argument there,'' Doc murmured. A moment later he gave a grunt. ''Look yonder! Somebody managed to make the riffle—unless that's the law comin'!''

Two unhurried figures could be seen advancing over the rolling swells. Doc and Wells peered carefully until the former thought he recognized one of their comrades. ''That's Gila!'' exclaimed Doc, with relief. ''Must be Chet with him—''

Once satisfied that they had nothing to fear from the newcomers, they showed themselves boldly. Gila waved without increasing his pace, and it was presently seen that he was laboriously assisting Denton. Climbing down the rocks, Harve and Doc moved out to meet the pair. Chet Denton's face was pasty. He had one thigh bound up, and Gila's expression was thunderous.

''What happened?'' Doc threw at them. ''We thought yuh was coverin' us, there in the street. Yuh plumb disappeared!''

''Dang good thing for you we did,'' Gila snapped. ''That blasted Towner showed up, Wells—an' who was with him but them hard-boiled old fools yuh hoisted on Rafe Alford's spread! The short, fat one recognized me an' let out a yell. The three of 'em was primed, and we couldn't stop 'em. The one-eyed galoot got Chet through the leg . . . But at least we led 'em off long enough for you to get in the clear—"

"Towner! Yuh mean *Gif* Towner—the U. S. marshal? There in Antler?" Doc was incredulous. Suddenly he whirled on Wells. "Dang it, Harve! So that's who yuh was talkin' about!" he burst out hoarsely. "Yuh knowed Towner was there all the time—an' wouldn't warn any of us!"

"You're crazy!" Harve rose to the occasion violently. "I didn't know anything of the kind, or I wouldn't've been there myself."

"I don't know, Harve," Gila said coldly. "I been wonderin' about you lately. Monkeyin' round that girl's made yuh altogether different—"

"And by the way," put in Denton wearily, dismounting with great care to ease his wounded leg, "what do yuh suppose happened to Stevens, boss?"

Harve made an impatient gesture. "Hell with him! I told yuh he couldn't even be bothered to watch the horses! He was gone ten minutes after we left him. Maybe he's drifted. Or," he continued meaningfully, "if Towner should happen to down him, and mistake him for me, that's all to the mustard too!"

They were staring at him, groping for his meaning, when the scrape and ring of iron hoofs just outside the rocky amphitheater froze them in their tracks. Then Doc ran to the mouth of the hollow, gun in hand. He fell back, jaw hanging slack, as Pat Stevens boldly rode in, followed by young MacEwen.

Stevens confronted them all with chill composure. He waited without a word for Harve Wells's reaction to his unexpected appearance. After the first unbelieving glare, the outlaw leader pulled himself together and showed great presence of mind.

"Well, now, Stevens!" He pretended severity. "I thought we'd seen the last of you—"

Pat's smile was wry. "I don't doubt it," he commented tersely. "But yuh wouldn't throw me down now, Wells. I was seen there in Antler. Recognized, too," he added pointedly. "That ought to be worth a little protection—even to you!"

The double meaning in Pat's words made the waiting outlaws hesitate. Doc abruptly remembered the curious business of Wells's bandana, there in the bank. He suddenly saw its significance now, given the resemblance between these men—but how could Stevens have guessed? On the other hand, they couldn't know what might have happened to him after they left. Doc's mouth flew open, ready to quiz Pat on that score. But Harve was already speaking:

"Just how would yuh explain your leavin' those horses last night?" he asked Pat ominously.

"Why, I was shot at and chased! Didn't you hear anything at all?" Pat put on a look of considerable innocence. "I was lucky to get away from there with my hide—and that's about all I *did* do."

"I wouldn't say that," put in MacEwen doggedly. He stared around at the others. "Stevens hauled me out of that street, boys, when I was ready to drop!" Whatever it might mean to them, he appeared convinced that Pat's action was responsible for his present freedom and safety. Dried blood still showed on his neck and jaw.

If Wells was conscious of Stevens's subtle revelation of treachery, during the scrambled affair in Antler, he betrayed nothing of it. All his irritation seemed concentrated on young Brad.

"Now that you're here, MacEwen," he rasped, "that was the craziest boner a man ever pulled—throwin' lead the way you done. We might never have got to our horses! . . . Was yuh deliberately tryin' to knock down our meat-house, or what was the object?"

Brad flushed, momentarily flustered. "Well, now, I wouldn't expect Doc to like that caper much—but *you* should understand," he retorted pointedly.

"Understand be damned!" Harve bawled, scarlet with fury. "I know that you hauled that town down around our ears by goin' off half-cocked! It'd served you right if Stevens had let yuh lay!"

MacEwen stared at him with blazing directness. "You didn't forget about Letty by any chance, did you, Harve?" he queried thinly. "She was still inside that bank, without a ghost of a chance to get away, after you made sure of your own skin!"

Taut silence followed these stinging words, broken only by the sound of Wells's angry breathing.

"There was certainly no need for anyone to worry on my account," a new voice suddenly struck in composedly. "Nor do I consider myself obligated to any of you, thanks!"

They whirled to find Letty sitting her saddle a few yards away, as if just returned from a leisurely ride. Gazing at her, Harve Wells's face showed his smug self-congratulation.

"Ha!" he exclaimed richly. "So yuh see how much need there was for makin' a fuss about her, boy!" He seemed doubly sure of his superior knowledge of the girl.

But young MacEwen glowered at Letty in obvious dismay. "You here?" he blurted in chagrin. "Blame it, Letty—don't you have enough sense to make for home?"

Clearly she did not accept his bluntness gracefully. "Have you ever asked me what I happened to think of your being here, Brad MacEwen?" she responded coolly.

Pat believed he knew the direction in which her mind was running, and it did not suit him to see the pair irritating each other so deliberately.

"Oh, come, now. She's bothered about her dad, of course," Pat inserted calmly. "And I can't say I blame her a whole lot . . . Have you made any particular arrangements for pickin' Grapes up?" he asked Wells bluntly.

Harve hadn't. For a second he could find nothing to say. It was not in him to worry unduly about others, but he was not anxious to betray the fact before Letty. Doc spoke up before Wells could meet the subtle challenge.

"By your tell, yuh was on the drift yourself last night," the bearded outlaw told Pat shrewdly. "Did yuh make it back to Ernie's camp, Stevens, or didn't yuh?"

"It happens I did." Pat was markedly dry. "Grapes was fretting about the rest of you, and he rode back to Antler with me early this morning. I left him outside of town—and then later I didn't see him again."

"What!" Wells evinced a towering disgust. "That was a fool move, Stevens—bringin' him to Antler! What did yuh think we left him behind for? Ernie ain't up to a fast ride. And with posses scourin' around after us, they'll scoop him up, sure as God made little apples!"

Pat shrugged. "Don't blame me. *You've* tried tellin'

Grapes what to do, yourself," he retorted easily. "It don't work."

They wrangled briefly while Letty listened, disturbed. They were interrupted almost at once by a gruff cry from Gila, who had climbed up the rocks after the girl's arrival to keep watch.

"Somebody out there in the brush, boss," the outlaw called warningly.

"How many?" Wells rifled back, tensing.

"Only one that I can see—about a mile away," was the reply.

They rushed to the rocks for a look, and it was Pat who first identified the man in the open. It was Sam Sloan, and Stevens was careful to show no recognition. "I'll just jog out there and lead that gent away," he began. But Harve halted him before he could climb down to his horse.

"No, yuh don't!" Wells bit the words off crisply. "You'll stay right where yuh are, mister!" After a moment's pondering he turned. "Doc, you're a smart operator . . . Show yourself a minute or two, an' then duck. Maybe we can coax that curious hombre close enough to grab him. I'd like to hear what he's got to say."

There was nothing to do, and Pat made no move to interfere with the cunning game. Doc did as directed. Sam saw him, and he appeared puzzled, scrutinizing the Lava Rocks with care. But he was keenly interested, and at length began a roundabout approach. Wells noted it with satisfaction.

"Okay, Doc! You and Gila grab him soon as he comes close enough—"

Stealthy and watchful, the pair moved away through the bewildering maze of rocks. It was long minutes before the others heard exasperated swearing, some distance beyond the lava barriers. At length Gila appeared, leading Sam's horse, with Doc in the rear holding a gun on the chunky man.

"Well, nosy!" Wells opened up offensively, studying their captive. "What would you be after?"

"You." Sam grinned wolfishly, looking them over boldly. If he took special note of Stevens, he failed to show it; but he examined the outlaw leader with particular care.

"You've found me." Abruptly Harve's tone took on an

edge. "Where's that Towner hombre yuh been travelin' with?"

Sam shrugged, waving a hand vaguely. "We split up. Gif's prowlin' the range somewheres. Looks now as if he should have stuck with me—"

Wells never took his hard eyes from the round, blue-stubbled face before him. "Don't lie, now! Towner wouldn't be haulin' Ernie Grapes off to the jug, would he?"

"Grapes?" Sloan appeared puzzled. "Why would he be doin' that?" His tone changed as he glimpsed Letty, and it may have been pretense that he failed to understand her presence here. "We did stumble over the old bird in camp last night," he acknowledged in a scoffing tone. "He passed his outfit off as ridin' roundup for Z-Bar-A—"

"*What* brand?" Doc thrust in, quickly and sharply. "The Zebra—?"

"Sounds like that, don't it?" Sam chuckled. "Z-Bar-A is what Grapes called it—"

Doc's guffaw was a grim bark. "Danged if I ever suspected the old duffer of that kind of humor. Zebra's a critter with stripes, ain't it? . . . Reckon Ernie meant we was ridin' the State's prison detail!" He lifted his brows at the end in half-comical protest.

"Well—it sounded all right," insisted Sam. "An' I reckon Gif didn't know Grapes from Adam. Anyway, we left him where we found him. Towner ain't interested in him," he asserted positively.

Some obscure force had been building up in Harve Wells as he listened, and at this he exploded: "You fool, Gif Towner's knowed Ernie Grapes from a boy! They've punched cows together, and it was Towner who finally put Grapes behind the bars a dozen years ago! . . . Don't even know him, don't he? Huh!"

Sam stared his surprise, oblivious of the low contempt evident in Harve's outburst. But it was Brad MacEwen who saw accurately the bitter significance of Wells's revelation.

"Blast you, Wells; why wasn't we told that days ago?" he asked accusingly. "You knew the risk Grapes ran, and yuh never let out a peep . . . Of *course* Towner's grabbed him by this time! Caught only a few miles from Antler, he'll be slapped with that bank robbery, sure as death; and he never had a thing to do with it!''

Every face in the circle revealed varying degrees of alarm or disgust, a fact which Harve could scarcely afford to ignore.

"Nonsense," he exclaimed forcibly. "He may even be on his way home by now! Stevens last saw him in the saddle—and Ernie ain't exactly a fool. Since you're so concerned, though," he told MacEwen flatly, "yuh can go hunt him up if yuh want. And don't lose no time about it, big mouth!''

Brad glared briefly. But he had no more to say. Turning away, he swung astride his bronc and jogged out of the rocks.

They watched him grow smaller across the range and finally fade from sight. All knew it might be a long wait, and Doc improved the time by brewing coffee and breaking out some food.

"Don't worry, Letty," Harve tried to pacify the girl, in his oily way. "MacEwen'll find your pa safe and sound, I'll bet on it!''

"Yes? It doesn't seem to have occurred to you that you're sending Brad where there is an excellent chance he may be picked up himself," the girl responded, an unusual tightness in her tone.

Harve could not miss the biting reproach in this. "But good Lord, girl! I'm only tryin' to please yuh," he protested. "Don't tell me you're fussin' yourself about that wet-eared kid now! . . . You're some strung up, I reckon," he proceeded with more assurance. "We're all edgy, for that matter. Forget it, now; and if Mac don't show up later in the day, we'll pull out for a safer place.''

But noon came and the afternoon dragged on, and watch as they would, Brad did not put in an appearance. Restless as Wells grew, he dared not try to crowd those in the bunch who were concerned for both Grapes and MacEwen.

Dusk gathered, and Harve was preparing himself for an ultimatum when the group was alerted by the clatter of racing hoofbeats. Moments later Brad MacEwen burst into their midst, hauling his mount in with a scatter of dirt.

"I was right, Wells—and you were wrong!" he hurled at the outlaw. "Less than an hour ago I watched Towner and half-a-dozen men herdin' Ernie Grapes into town! He's in jail right now! What do yuh think of that?''

11.

NEWS OF ERNIE GRAPES'S capture was received with varying degrees of interest. Letty went white in the flickering glow from the campfire, and Doc muttered softly into his beard. In Gila's tense face could be read relief that it was not himself. Harve Wells was only annoyed.

"Too bad," he growled. "Ern's gettin' too old to stay on his toes. But like MacEwen said," he continued evenly, "they can't prove a thing on him."

"Do they need to?" Brad's look was scornful. "Accordin' to you, Towner was only waitin' to clamp down on the man! He won't miss a trick—"

Harve listened scowling to this argument. He shrugged. "So what can *we* do?" he countered, shortly and sourly.

"You could've left him alone in the first place," MacEwen tossed back flatly. "But no—yuh had to have Grapes with us! Dammit, man, the least yuh can do now is get up on your hocks and spring the old boy!" He looked anxiously about at the other faces for confirmation.

Wells threw his head up, his jaw set stubbornly. "Unh-uh! Nothin' doin'," he vetoed finally. "Left to himself, Ern's got a bare chance to wriggle out of this. Spring him, and it'll look like proof that he's guilty." He smugly stated the argument relieving himself of responsibility. He stopped then, his glance sharpening. "What's your stake in this anyhow, MacEwen? Grapes is an older hand than any of us. He knows how to look after himself, and it's my opinion he'll be back with us in no time."

If he said this for Letty's benefit, it failed signally to impress the others. Pat Stevens was little inclined to let him get away with any such smooth and meaningless talk.

"And I say he won't," Pat said boldly. "By your own

authority, Wells, Marshal Towner has watched Grapes for years. Whatever the local law decides, Gif could throw one charge after another at Grapes—even tie him down for life!''

Harve exhibited growing impatience with this attack from all sides. He eyed Pat coldly for a space as if making up his mind. His reply was deliberate.

''You keep hangin' around, Stevens, like a blasted deer-fly,'' he brought out flatly. ''Yuh got plenty to say, too—but I ain't noticed that yuh've done much.'' His pause was a challenge. ''Show us what you're made of—you're such a hotshot. Go and get Grapes, and maybe we'll change our minds about you!''

Whether or not Pat had expected something of the kind, it failed to disturb him. It took him only a matter of seconds to weigh the cynical proposal and come to a decision. To the surprise of all he nodded.

''I'll do that,'' he declared coldly. ''If only to prove I know a trick or two, Harve, that you're afraid to tackle—''

Wells scowled at the jibe. Since his unsuccessful attack on the other's life, he had noticed a growing insolence in Pat's behavior, and didn't know just how to take it. He kept a grip on himself, and even managed a sneering retort.

''Still working your jaw overtime, I see,'' he said stiffly. ''Wouldn't be meant to impress Letty, would it?''

Pat turned to face the girl with radically changed manner. ''Don't you worry, ma'am,'' he advised quietly. ''I know how Brad feels, and I expect you agree with him to an extent. I'll do what I can, of course, short of makin' any serious mistake. If it's humanly possible to haul your dad out of his jam, we'll manage somehow.''

''Ver-ry pretty,'' commented Harve sardonically, playing for an audience. His laugh was mean. But it could not prevent Pat from noting the flash of earnest thanks in the girl's worried eyes. Nor did Brad MacEwen bother to mask his true sentiments.

''Good for you, Stevens! You're the right stuff,'' he said approvingly. ''In fact, I'm prepared to go along with yuh—''

But Pat shook his head. ''Thanks, Mac. Could be I'll

wish you had, before I'm done with this. Right now I aim
to go it alone, though. I've got an idea that may work. If I
lose, at least I'll be the only one—and then, if it still
bothers yuh, you can take it from there.''

He turned to his bronc as he finished, wrenched the
cinch tight, and swung astride without more words.

"Shall we look for yuh before mornin', Stevens?'' Wells
could not forego the malicious dig.

"You can look for me when I get back." Pat was curt.
"And I will be, Wells. You might as well resign yourself
to it!"

Giving a last, meaningful look, he moved unhurriedly
out of the circle of light and a few moments later was gone
from sight and hearing.

He well knew the risk he ran in approaching Antler so
soon after the robbery. Towner would probably be in
town, grilling his captive, but the local sheriff undoubtedly
had a posse or two out. In the darkness Pat might, with
care, be able to avoid these. Yet would he be any better
off, once he had reached Antler? The federal marshal
would not overlook the possibility of precisely what Brad
MacEwen had proposed—a raid designed to free Grapes—
and would be prepared to meet it.

Pat's sole advantage was that he wanted to meet the
lawman face to face. That way lay his only hope of
success.

In town, he left his pony at the same shed which once
before had nearly proved fatal for him. He took to a side
street, and, moving without haste in the enveloping dark,
angled into the open yards before reaching the main drag.
An alley led to the corner of a livery barn and here Pat
paused undecided, finally yanking his hat down and moving toward the wide gangway door.

A hostler who was hitching up a ranch rig just inside
offered scant attention as Pat accosted him.

"Is Marshal Towner lookin' for any more men, Jack?"

"Don't know. Whyn't yuh ask him, buster?"

Pat grunted. "I'm tryin' to find him now—"

"Well, he *was* stayin' at the boardin'house," came the
retort. "What kind of a posseman d'you think you'd make,
anyhow?"

Pat's chuckle was perfunctory. "Thanks, Jack," he turned away.

He had what he wanted. Five minutes later he stole toward the rear of the boardinghouse, scanning the lights visible in a number of rear windows. A kitchen door stood invitingly open, but beyond could be heard the clatter of a busy cook cleaning up after supper. Pat moved on. A dog growled and sniffed at his bootleg. A subdued clucking of Stevens's tongue caused him to lose interest.

There was another door at the side, closed and dark now. Peering in from the porch, Pat made sure the room beyond was empty. The doorknob turned in his grasp, there was a faint jar, and he was inside. He found himself in a gloomy side-parlor. Stepping through a rustling bead curtain, he reached the hallway. Ten quiet steps took him to the stairs, and he sprang lightly up them.

The second-story hall of this sizable place was built in the form of an ell. As he reached the top, Pat heard a murmuring of masculine voices not far away.

The hall was dim, lighted by a single oil lamp. Reaching the turn, Stevens jarred to a halt. Three or four armed men were standing, heads together, near an open door through which light streamed. It was their voices he heard. It hit him, moreover, that Gif Towner must even now be in that room, just beyond his reach.

For ten seconds Pat weighed his chances of reaching the man without being stopped, and decided on a bold course. Moving forward confidently, he strode past the men, who broke off their talk to stare at him, and made straight for the inner doorway.

"Hey! Don't yuh barge in there—"

Ignoring the exclamation, Pat reached the opening and moved on through. He was right about one thing. Marshal Towner was indeed here in the guarded room. It would hardly have startled Pat to find Ezra with him, following the disappearance of Sam Sloan. But such was not the case. The man conferring absorbedly with Towner, a stranger, might have been a bank or town official, from his looks.

Hearing Pat's boots, Gif whirled impatiently in his chair.

"What now! I thought I told yuh—" Glimpsing Pat, he broke off abruptly. "Oh. You, is it?" he grunted.

"Yes, Towner. It's me."

Towner rose slowly to his feet, measuring Stevens with cold aloofness. It was a moment before he spoke. "We'll call it off for now, Mingus," he said heavily. "I want to talk to this man."

His visitor sprang up as if insulted, and stared at Pat without a sign of recognition. "Well! I reckon your time's your own—" Grabbing his hat, he started to turn away.

"Just close the door after yuh, please," Towner requested, his eyes not leaving Pat's face. The door shut with a bang, leaving them alone.

"Well, Stevens, you've got brass. I'll say that for you!" Gif opened up tartly.

"How so?" Pat pretended surprise. "After all, Towner, we made a deal. You must have expected some kind of a report sooner or later," he pointed out smoothly.

"You're too late—I know mighty well what's been goin' on." The lawman seemed gloomy over his thoughts. "By the way, Stevens. Ever lay eyes on that gent I was talkin' to when yuh busted in here?" he demanded casually.

Pat appeared to search his mind. "Can't say I have." He shook his head. "Why?"

"Yuh just passed a stiff test—whether yuh know it or not." Gif was clearly annoyed at having to admit this. "That was Rad Mingus, from the bank, Stevens . . . He stood face to face with them holdups, this mornin'. He's already given me a pretty close description of Harve Wells. If *he* didn't recognize yuh—and from his actions I'd swear he didn't—then yuh can't be one of 'em, after all."

Pat chuckled. "Told you I wasn't," he commented lightly. "Someday you'll learn to listen, Towner . . . Right now I'm here to talk about someone besides myself."

"That so?" Gif frowned. "Wouldn't be Wells himself, would it?"

"Indirectly." Smiling, Pat knew the other was sparring. "But mainly, Marshal, it's about Ernie Grapes."

"Yeh, we got him." Towner nodded without batting an eye. "One of Harve's long-riders—"

"No, Towner. He isn't," Stevens contradicted flatly.

Gif declined to take the bait, but his rocky face set in hard lines. "We think he is."

Pat shook his head slowly and firmly. "You don't think anything of the kind. Because, Towner, you know different!"

Gif stared, caught. His jaw reddened. "Do I—?"

"I happen to know that you two are acquainted," Pat proceeded levelly. "Well acquainted. He's on parole in your care, Marshal—and if you've got any idea in your head that he's thrown yuh down, you're dead wrong."

"Well, now—" Gif began argumentatively.

"Askin' for proof, is that it?" Pat put on a confident front. "Okay. Have Grapes brought up here, Towner. You've got the authority for that. And I'll lay it on the line!"

The lawman stalled stubbornly, but at Pat's insistence he finally relented. "Ernie wouldn't talk for me, Stevens. Maybe he will for you." Going to the door, he gave terse instructions to one of the men in the hall. They waited ten minutes, and Pat had time to roll a smoke, before boots shuffled outside and the door opened to admit Grapes.

Darting a swift look at them, Ernie halted just inside the door and stood with head lowered.

"There yuh are, Stevens—" Towner waited, his look stern yet curious.

Pat nodded. "What have you got against this man, Towner?"

Gif was succinct. "Ridin' with Harve Wells."

"What would that mean—if anything? Grapes was nowhere near that train holdup. I know, because I was with him myself. And he wasn't in on the bank job, any more than I was!"

Gif was very serious and showed resentment. "Next yuh'll be tellin' me he wasn't even ridin' with Wells, Stevens, and I know better!"

"So what? *I'm* ridin' with Harve, too—for a purpose. How do yuh know Ernie hasn't got fully as good a one?"

Gif weighed this briefly before shaking his head with a frown. But Pat had succeeded in arousing Grapes's interest. The latter glanced uneasily his way, and pricked up his ears.

"What would it be?" the lawman growled skeptically.

Pat delayed a few seconds for effect. "Letty Grapes is with Harve Wells right this minute," he said. "Ernie was there on her account, Towner, and nothin' else!"

Gif started up sharply, his eyes hard, and then sank back slowly. He was more suspicious than ever. "Are yuh tellin' me that Wells kidnapped the girl, Stevens?"

Pat grinned. "Harve more or less thinks he has," he returned. "It was Letty's chance, and she grabbed it."

"Her chance—?" Towner was puzzled. "I don't get yuh."

Pat coolly revealed Wells's determined attempt to drag Grapes back into outlawry, and how the old rawhide had blocked this by letting his horse throw him. Gif listened intently, but Ernie himself displayed gathering disgust.

"Do yuh have to tell everything yuh know, Stevens?" he burst out abruptly.

Pat turned a smile on him. "Then why didn't you tell Towner your story?" he countered.

"An' get laughed at?" Grapes snorted. "The old hardshell probably don't even believe it now—"

Towner regarded him steadily. "Has he got it straight?" His tone was mild. "Is that how it was, Ern?"

Grapes glowered. "Well, I been tryin' hard t' keep Letty out o' trouble. That's true enough!"

"I see." Towner rubbed his prominent jaw thoughtfully. "Everything but that girl's object, that is . . . Why *is* she stickin' with Wells, Stevens?" His eyes narrowed.

"His name's Brad MacEwen." Pat chuckled. "Good lookin' young rip, Towner. A little wild, maybe. I don't think he's an out-and-out owlhoot."

"*What!*" Grapes was staring, astounded. "Yuh mean she's interested in young Brad—? How— What—" He broke off, unable to express himself.

Pat's brows raised. "Good Lord, Grapes! You mean you didn't know?" But even he could not mistake the relief and happiness flooding over Ernie's whole face, mingled with a fresh bewilderment. "Just how dumb can a father be?"

"MacEwen." Gif Towner pondered. "I know a little about him . . . And Letty's tryin' to pry MacEwen away from Wells's gang. Is that it, Stevens?"

"I thought you'd tumble." Pat nodded approvingly. "That's the picture. And a mighty sour one for a couple of mixed-up kids, unless things change mighty quick!"

"And so you're tryin' to help out, I expect." Towner was quizzical. "What do yuh suggest, Stevens?"

"Turn Grapes loose," said Pat promptly. "In my custody if you insist. Between us we'll straighten those youngsters out."

"Nope." Gif spoke promptly and decidedly. "There's a train been stuck up, Stevens, and a bank robbed. I'm here to grab the men who did it, an' nothin' else!"

"I promised to help turn Wells in," Pat urged gently. But the lawman was not to be budged an inch.

"No sir! Absolutely nothin' doin'." Calculation crept into his tone. "Tell yuh what, though. Yuh know where that gang is holed up. Take me there now, and Grapes can go along."

Pat sat forward, and hesitated. "No posse, though. I won't risk a lot of reckless killin', Towner. If we can grab that bunch by ourselves, all right."

There was further hard-headed discussion, but this was Pat's last word. Towner was too anxious to risk losing this chance, and he relented. Grapes signified his willingness to accompany them, if his daughter's safety was assured; and in the end Towner jumped up, ready to go.

"We're off," he grunted. "And there better be results!"

The people of Antler were considerably surprised as the three prepared to shove off. But Towner's federal authority served its purpose, and no one interfered with them.

"Where we goin'?" Gif growled bluntly as the lights of town dwindled to the rear.

"Lava Rocks," Pat informed him frankly. "The bunch has been layin' out there all day, Towner."

Gif swore disgustedly. "An' I was in sight of the place, too! We couldn't spot no tracks . . . Come on—give them broncs the gaff!"

They rode swiftly, the miles dropping behind. Approaching the ragged silhouette against the stars, Pat searched the shadowy volcanic ruin in vain for signs of a fire. He moved from side to side, and began to slow down. Towner stared at him sharply in the gloom.

"What's the matter?"

"Damned if I don't think they've pulled up stakes on us, Marshal, bag and baggage!" Pat whipped out. He urged his pony forward.

It was only too true. They reached the rocky hollow presently to find it abandoned and silent, although there were plenty of signs that the outlaws had been here. Wells and his hardcases were gone, and with them all traces of Sam, Letty and MacEwen.

12.

IF GIF TOWNER had had his differences with Sam Sloan and Ezra, he had watched them long enough to be satisfied that they were not outlaws. The trio had parted company in Antler with no hard feelings; with the bank holdup Towner found himself involved in a whirlwind of detail, and it would have surprised the lawman to learn that the long-legged redhead had taken the trouble to follow him, Pat and Ernie Grapes at a discreet distance to Lava Rocks.

Ezra had a triple purpose in trailing along as he did. For one thing he was hunting for Sam, who had disappeared during the course of the afternoon; and for another, he was deeply curious to learn where Pat Stevens might be leading the federal marshal. Lastly, Ezra suspected shrewdly that, wherever they might be going, Harve Wells would not be far away—and ever since being relieved of the Bar ES horse money, Ez had hankered keenly for a meeting with the outlaw leader.

Having approached Lava Rocks cautiously, Stevens and the marshal lit brush torches and prowled about investigating, while Grapes waited. Watching from a distance, Ezra concluded rightly that if Wells's gang had been hiding here it was gone now. Losing interest after a time, he withdrew to a safe distance in the brush and prepared to camp. Tomorrow promised to be a busy day for him, and as things stood he didn't want to meet with anyone likely to give him an argument.

He was soon asleep, and was not disturbed during the dark hours. Early dawn found him sizing up the morning and getting ready to move on. Evidently he had the empty range to himself. Strict economy of energy characterized his preparations, and from his preoccupied air his thoughts were already busy.

Lava Rocks had at one time been a volcanic cone. Eroded and broken down, it was surrounded for thousands of yards by an area of crumbling, pulverized lava and cinders that withstood any imprint of a horse's hoof. Methodically Ezra found his way to the outer edge of this hard ground and began to follow it in a circular path through the endless brush.

He rode along, his single eye alert, then stopped abruptly. A single set of tracks appeared, striking directly away from the rocks. Ez followed, only to find where they joined other tracks and looped back into the lava field. Sticking to the soft soil, he pushed on patiently. Fifteen minutes later he had better luck. The clear sign of eight or ten horses emerged from the lava at one point and struck into the west.

This trail did not turn. It ran straight on, and the lanky tracker made no doubt that Wells's gang had ridden this way. Climbing a rise a mile farther on, he delayed to sweep the horizon. No sign of life showed anywhere, and this he found hard to understand.

"Towner must be a little stupid," he thought sourly. "If he wants t' nab Wells, why ain't he ridin' this way now?"

Concerned about his partner's absence, he would not wait. If the outlaws had grabbed Sam, as seemed only too possible, the stocky man would even now be awaiting help, and Ezra meant to supply it.

The track led on into the west, as if the owlhoots were in no doubt of their objective. Before midday the first rising hog-back slopes of the Rockies came into view. Probably Wells was striking out for a hideout in the hills.

An hour later the rocky heights loomed close. Ez trailed the gang past a lofty butte and saw that their course continued directly on toward a deep cleft between two other buttes. Before long, gazing down a long tawny slope he saw the weathered buildings of a tiny village, jumbled together in the throat of the granite gap.

Drawing rein, Ezra gazed that way long and speculatively. "That must be Canyon," he mused. It gave him pause because for years the town had borne an unsavory reputation. "That could be Harve Wells's headquarters. An' danged if I don't think it is, by gum!"

In company with Stevens or Sam Sloan, Ez would have made nothing of riding boldly into the place and bluffing it out. Alone, he knew better. Leaving the trail he had followed for miles, he dropped from sight in a wash and circled wide, to reach the wall of the rising hog-back and follow it unhurriedly toward Canyon. Like broken bones the red rocks slanted up out of the earth, leaving gaps and hollows between the worn strata. Clinging to these, Ez won to a vantage point not more than a couple of hundred yards from the town. Climbing a crumbling ledge, he peered long and narrowly toward the cluster of buildings.

There was little to be seen. A man crossed the dusty street and disappeared into a store. Two or three saddle horses switched flies. There was no other evidence of life. But Ezra had sensed danger in the very absence of movement, his years of experience having taught him to seek deception first in such towns as this. Laboriously he worked closer, scrutinizing the run-down buildings for any information they might yield.

After a long delay another man appeared on the porch of a saloon. At this distance Ez could not make out his features, but the other paused to give the outspread plains a wary glance. Ezra saw that this was no man with an easy conscience, whatever else he was. Presently the other led a horse into the street, and the big fellow stiffened.

"I've lamped that bronc before! On the Rafter A, I reckon." He nodded to himself. "Looks t' me like one o' Wells's crowd. Wonder where he's goin'?"

Mounting, the man struck out of town at a brisk trot and headed back into the hills. Ez dropped from his perch and ran to his pony. It put him to no little trouble to circle around Canyon without being seen, and by the time he succeeded the man he had been watching had disappeared completely from sight.

In disgust, Ezra cast about for the fellow's tracks and shortly picked them up where they turned into a kind of dim trail. The way wound on through several rocky gaps and angled south into rough country. Too smart to make the mistake of hurrying, Ez had just settled himself for another long ride when he spied the roof of a building not far ahead, partly hidden by a nearby rise. He approached with care.

A run-down, dilapidated building, which once must have been a ranch house, stood on a gravelly flat. Ez looked it over dubiously, and rode quietly on.

Two rough-looking men were seated on the porch steps as Ezra came deliberately forward. They broke off their low-voiced talk and stared steadily in his direction. The rough trail wound on past the place, and they watched him jog by.

By no means sure he recognized either of the men, at the same time Ezra felt strongly confident that he had finally unearthed the stronghold of the outlaw gang. Cliff-walled peaks rose on every hand, and it would have been hard to find a more remote spot. Eyeing the shuttered windows, he was almost certain that even now Sam Sloan was being held there.

He neither paused nor spoke as he passed on down the trail; but a few minutes later he was circling the place circumspectly. If he spotted Sam's bronc in the corral at the rear, he told himself, he would know for sure.

No horses at all were visible in the broken corral. They might be held in the nearby sagging shed. But another man was leaning indolently against the rear wall of the house, a rifle propped near at hand. Ez eyed him bleakly, drawing rein for an instant of indecision. Then he pressed coolly forward.

"Stop where yuh are, stranger." The guard halted him a dozen feet away.

Ezra reined down, looking about him casually. "What place is this, anyhow?" he queried.

There was no reply.

"Huh!" Ezra pretended mild scorn. "Cat got your tongue, mister? . . . I ain't after nothin' but a little information."

Still there was no response. The flinty eyes watched him steadily.

"Pah!" Ezra's disgust grew. "Hard hombre, ain't yuh? Couple fellers out front that probably ain't as shy as you—"

He circled the house with apparent indolence, though he was, in reality, very uneasy. The pair on the front porch half-started to their feet as he appeared.

"Nosy jasper," one of them muttered. But they only watched his unhurried advance.

"Howdy, boys." Ez reined in with an air of frankness. "Lookin' for a friend o' mine. Maybe he come this way—"

"He ain't here." The reply was threatening and final.

Ez ignored it, his brows lifting. "How could yuh know? Ain't described him yet." He was both stubborn and ingenuous. "About my height. Two hundred pounds, maybe. Blue eyes—name of Ace Brown." He was reeling off random details as they came to mind.

"He ain't here. Go 'long, now."

Instead Ezra coolly dismounted. "Well, somehow I got the notion he's inside. Ain't that queer? Reckon yuh won't mind if I just take a look—"

A stalwart form blocked his path. Blazing pupils bored into his.

"Are yuh goin'?"

"Oh, come on now!" Ez began cajolingly. Before he could get another word out, powerful hands seized him. Never had he felt such gorilla strength as took him in charge now. He was shaken and tumbled about till his teeth rattled, and sailed finally through the air to bounce with a spine-bruising jolt on the ground a dozen feet away.

Even now Ez did not altogether lose his head. He stumbled up, jaw quivering, and didn't have to pretend his astonishment and rage. "Real tough boy, you are—!"

"Pull your freight, grampa."

Breathing loudly, Ezra grabbed his bridle and scrambled into the saddle, suppressing a grimace of pain as he did so. Stiffly, without another glance, he turned the horse and rode deliberately down the trail. Before he had covered a dozen yards his thoughts were churning busily.

"That bunch ain't t' be got around," he mused gloomily. "But they got Sam in there. I'm sure of it! . . . What'll I do now?"

Not till the sinister ranch house had dropped from sight to the rear did he dare slacken his pace. The idea came to him that he might watch the place, but he knew it was useless. What he needed was help. It would take long hours to return to Antler for Gif Towner, and for once Ezra found himself completely stumped.

Morosely he pushed on, riding indifferently into the little owlhoot town, scarcely caring what might happen. He was hauling up before the rattletrap saloon, looking neither to right or left, when a harsh voice accosted him, startlingly close.

"Drinkin' again, eh? Put up your hands. You're under arrest for bein' alive!"

Ez jerked around violently to find himself staring into the grinning face of Pat Stevens. The latter had walked across the street from his standing horse, and glancing that way Ez saw Ernie Grapes waiting, still astride. Relief flooded over him. A matter of hours ago he had deliberately avoided the pair; now their meeting seemed nothing short of providential.

"Holy smoke, Stevens! Where yuh been? I been lookin' all over for yuh—"

"That so?" Ignoring the prevarication, Pat read the other shrewdly and accurately. "Thought yuh were lookin' for Sam—"

"I have been—an' what's more, I found him, too!" Ez blurted.

Pat's eyes widened. Instantly recognizing the seriousness in this, he lowered his voice. "Come over here and tell us about it, Ez."

The redhead lost no time telling Pat and Grapes about his experience at the isolated house in the hills. He was positive it was Harve Wells's headquarters. "An' they're holdin' Sam there. They must be," Ez wound up.

Pat nodded. "They've got him. Or did have. I'm afraid you'll have to join him for a while, Ez. You're takin' us there, of course."

Ez looked crestfallen. "Where's Towner? Ain't he with yuh—?"

Pat's smile was disparaging. "Afraid we'll have to get along without his help."

Quick on the up-take, Ez shrugged. "Let's get about it, then," he growled.

It took them twenty minutes to come to the isolated

house on the flat. The guards stood up to stare first at
Ernie Grapes, and then at Pat.

"Sufferin' succotash, Stevens!" Chet Denton burst out
incredulously. "How'd yuh manage to pry him loose—?"
He jerked his chin toward Grapes.

Pat's glance as he dismounted was composed. "Harve
here?" He started coolly for the door.

"Yeh. He's inside." They made room for the new
arrivals to pass, completely ignoring Ezra, whom Pat thrust
on ahead of him.

Rumbling voices greeted them from the only good-sized
room in the place, and here the gang sat or stood about a
battered table behind which stood Harve Wells. His face
slowly froze at sight of Stevens.

"Well! Made it, did yuh?" It was said diffidently, and
his nod to Grapes was almost casual.

"We made it, Harve." Pat's thin smile had something
derisive in it.

"Where's Letty, Wells?" Old Ernie was staring about
the smoky room suspiciously. His query was gruff.

"She prefers an upstairs room—" Harve sounded
indulgent.

"Well, I'm goin' up an' see for myself."

Harve halted him before he could turn away. "Just a
minute, Ern." His voice turned hard. "You're back—but I
aim to know how Stevens worked it. Did he claw yuh out
of that hencoop jail . . . or was there some sort of a deal
with Towner?"

Grapes abruptly stilled, and stared at him with a face of
granite. It was impossible to tell what was going through
his mind, but no one could have missed the ugly inference
in Harve's cynical words.

"Find out your own way," the old rawhide exclaimed
defiantly. "Stevens done somethin' you wouldn't even try!
Yuh wanted me ridin' with yuh. Are yuh satisfied, or ain't
yuh?"

"No offense, Ern. Just a matter of curiosity—"

A flat silence fell as Grapes stumped from the room,
limping a little, and clumped up the shaking stairs. Harve
broke it by leveling a stern finger at Ezra.

"That's another of them Powder Valley bird-dogs, Stevens! Maybe yuh can explain bringin' him here," he rifled angrily.

Pat shrugged. They had no means of tracing the relationship between himself and Ez. He was safe there. "I found him nosin' around the place, Wells, and dragged him in. You did the same thing with another of 'em at Lava Rocks, didn't yuh?"

"That's so, boss." Denton spoke up. "I throwed the old terrapin off the place an hour ago. He was alone then—"

Wells grunted sourly. "All right, all right. Toss him in the back room with the fat party."

Ezra was hustled unceremoniously away.

"What would yuh want with those hombres?" inquired Pat.

Wells scowled. Before he could reply, Doc broke into the talk, burning with impatience.

"Oh hell, Harve! All this palaver still don't settle the argument here." He sounded stern. "I tell yuh we're all mighty unpopular, after that bank hoist. Gila voted we split the money and drift. Yuh wouldn't say yes, and yuh wouldn't say no. We want an answer."

The others pressed forward, waiting. It was all too plain that unceasing worry gnawed at them. None approved Wells's dragging a girl around in their wake, nor could they see sense or safety in his brazen tactics. They wanted out, and the outlaw leader's blustering air of surprise betrayed that he guessed their bitter mood correctly.

"Danged if that ain't gratitude!" he burst out scathingly. "I'm buildin' up a fat killin' for us all, if you hot-headed fools'll only hold your horses!"

It suited Pat's purpose to back him in this strategy of delay. "Easy, boys," he advised, smoothly and authoritatively. "Wells is undoubtedly right. Split the gravy now, and it'll probably slip through our fingers while we're making our getaway."

Gila whirled on him savagely. "Where the hell do you fit in this, mister?" he bit out. "Yuh may've done Grapes a favor, or made it look that way; but I ain't so sure that includes us. Yuh never lifted a finger t' earn any of this money we're dividin' up. Yuh flit back an' forth, an' talk mighty biggety—just who are you, anyway?" It was the most determined attack yet leveled at Pat, and it did not end there. "You're altogether too chummy with Gif Towner to suit me. Damned if I don't think you're a spy!"

He had his hand on his gun as he spat the bitter words, but that could not save him. There was a blur at Pat's hip as his Colt roared thunderously. Gila sprang erect, with a look of panic. Lips fluttering, his eyes glazed, and he wilted to the floor with a sodden thump. It was over in a second.

Wells lurched forward to peer over the table's edge. Seeing his own advantage in the suddenness of Gila's demise, he was smugly pleased.

"Reckon Gila asked for that," he said, his voice breaking the silence.

13.

"ANYBODY ELSE think I'm a rat?" Pat gave them all a menacing glare, his smoking sixgun ready.

There were no takers. Gradually tension left the outlaws. They straightened, faces stony. They had seen death before and all knew that survival depended on themselves alone.

Doc eyed Pat in a very different manner. "Yuh answered a lot of questions that time, Stevens." He was gruff, and if his reply was cryptic it seemed to satisfy Pat.

Steps clattered on the stairs and Ernie Grapes came hurrying down. "What kind o' doin's is this, with a girl around?" he bellowed. His eye picked up Gila, inert on the floor, and his glance at Pat, while it failed to linger, was strangely expressive.

"Too bad, Ern." Wells was authoritative. "Can't be helped—an' there won't be no more . . . Tell her I'm all right."

A queer look appeared on Grapes's face at this. But it appeared to silence him. Brad MacEwen turned his back, choking as he cleared his throat. Harve noticed nothing unusual.

"A couple of you boys carry Gila out and plant him," he directed callously.

Denton stepped forward, and MacEwen offered to help as if glad to get outside. They watched Gila being carried to his grave without comment. Pat did not even look that way, and Wells likewise appeared preoccupied.

"Reckon I'll question that one-eyed hombre that Stevens grabbed," he decided, rising to his feet. "He may be able to tell us somethin'."

Pat drifted to the sagging porch and sat down, noting

that the others studiously gave him plenty of elbow-room. He was not greatly concerned about either Ezra or Sam. The pair could be depended on to fend Wells off. Knowing Pat was not far away, they would play his game to the hilt.

It was late afternoon when, their task finished, Chet and MacEwen returned. Observing the latter pottering about the barn alone, Pat strolled down there.

"Well, Brad—"

MacEwen turned worried eyes on him. "How are we goin' to get Letty out of this, Stevens?" he demanded in a low voice.

Pat shrugged. "Maybe she'll leave when she's had enough." He was cautiously feeling the other out.

"But, hang it, this is serious!" exclaimed Brad. "It's been hell for me—"

"So?" Pat asked. "Then why not do something about it yourself?"

"But I—" MacEwen broke off, tongue-tied.

"Has it struck you that she'll be glad to leave when you do?" Pat persisted.

Brad was suddenly scarlet. "I may've guessed as much," he mumbled. "That's a lot different from knowin', Stevens!"

"Not taking any chances, eh?" Pat grew engaging. "Just what is the attraction here, boy? Like this life, do yuh?"

"I hate it," MacEwen burst out vehemently, only to check himself. "But what's the difference? What are yuh talkin' this way for? . . . Letty's got no more use for me than she has for Wells, if he only knew it, the fat-headed fool!"

It sounded hollow even to himself, but Brad would have pursued the theme with energy had not Wells himself appeared at that moment.

Strangely enough he found nothing remarkable in the guarded conference between the pair. He waved them forward impatiently and they were presently joined by Doc and Chet Denton.

"What's up, Harve?" The bearded outlaw watched the leader curiously.

"It's Letty." Wells jerked his head toward the house.

"She's raisin' the roof about Gila . . . I don't know whether I'm obliged to yuh or not, Stevens. She's even givin' her pa a hard time—"

"Hell, that's easy to settle." Doc came to the point. "Get rid of her!"

Harve snorted. "An' get rid of Grapes at the same time? He'll be the makin' of this crowd yet," he insisted dogmatically. "No—she's seen too many rough men for too long," he went on soberly. "I told her she could have a little trip to town. She'll be gone for a day or so."

"Where to? Canyon—or Antler?" Doc demanded with his usual skepticism.

"No, Dutch Springs is only fifty or sixty miles. She's known there, an' won't be specially noticed."

"Dutch Springs? Why, I've hung out there myself. I'll take her for you, Wells, and get her back," Pat offered. He wanted a talk with the girl, and would welcome this opportunity.

Harve's smile was pitying. "You poor sap, *you're* one of her big reasons for wantin' to get away—although she does a certain amount of talkin' about dress-goods . . . No, I'm takin' Letty to Dutch Springs personally," he informed them matter-of-factly. "It'll ease things all around, and yuh can look for us back the day after tomorrow, at the latest."

"What about Gif Towner?" Denton barked.

Wells showed his teeth briefly. "Don't fret about me," he retorted. "If we should happen to meet, you can start worryin' about him—"

At his instructions a battered ranch rig was rolled out of the shed and two broncs fastened in the traces. Mounting to the spring seat, Wells swung around before the house. After a moment Letty came sailing out of the door, her head held high. Old Ernie followed her, pleading. Harve restrained the horses long enough for her to clamber in. They started off with a jerk.

Scarcely were they beyond earshot before young MacEwen pitched hotly into Grapes. "Ain't you got no control at all over her?" he stormed. "Blamed if I approve for a second of her goin' off with him!"

His scorn was large. Instead of striking fire, however, it

humbled Ernie. "Think yuh'd have any better luck?" he grumbled morosely.

There seemed nothing more to be said. A close watch was kept, Doc smoothly taking charge without protest from the others. Pat would have liked to discuss the situation with Grapes, but he knew enough to leave the old-timer alone for the time being.

Evening closed in, Denton got supper for them, and the night dragged on. "Would yuh say we shook Towner, there in Antler, Stevens?" Doc inquired. He had assumed a pleasanter attitude toward Pat, and seemed anxious for the answer.

Pat's laugh was careless. "Only Towner can tell us that," he rejoined dryly.

"Well, then—are we safe here, like Harve thinks?"

"Where *are* we safe, Doc? Can you tell me that?" Pat was wary of friendship from this man. With a smile on his face he was doubly dangerous.

Aware of Pat's reserve, the bearded man persisted for some time, endeavoring to break down the other's coolness. "You're smart, Stevens—I seen that from the start. Wells hasn't got a thing on you. It could be," Doc hinted flatteringly, "that you an' I could get further together than he ever will—"

Pat received this coldly. "Watch your tongue, man. How can you be sure that talk won't get back to Wells?" A moment later he rose yawning. "I'm goin' to hit the hay."

Pushing into the small back room where a guard watched Sam and Ezra, he looked them over briefly. Far from sleepy, they were playing cards desultorily with a greasy deck and they hardly glanced at him.

"Better call one of us, Denton, if yuh begin to doze." Pat turned away.

It was long past sunrise before anyone was astir in the morning. An hour later Stevens found Ernie Grapes seated on a corral bar, gazing moodily down the trail.

"Keepin' an eye peeled for Gif?" he queried easily.

Ernie's answer was a grunt.

Doc amused himself trying to pump Ezra and Sam, but he got nowhere. Noon came and the sun beat down brilliantly on the empty flat. Pat took his turn guarding the pair, warning them silently to be patient.

Grapes rambled upstairs in midafternoon for a nap, taciturn as ever. The crunch of wheels an hour later brought him racketing down the stairs at a surprising speed. Without speaking to Pat or Doc, he rushed to the door and stopped.

The pair moved up behind him for a look. A glance sufficed to inform them what had brought him up so sharply. Harve Wells was coming, tooling the rig into the yard. And except for himself, the vehicle was empty.

Waiting, Grapes stepped out as Wells came walking up from the barn. "Well!" It was a challenging bark. "Where's my girl, you?"

Harve lifted heavy eyes, seeming somehow discouraged. "She'll be back," he hedged wearily.

"She will, huh? Why ain't she with yuh? Where is she right now?" Ernie fired his questions forcefully. "Blast it, Wells, you're so sure of havin' the inside track with Letty—what've yuh done with her, anyhow?"

The outlaw flushed. "Said she'd be back, didn't I?" he flared hotly. "Keep your shirt on, Ern! She—she insisted on doin' some fool errands, and I decided to—clear out of town." He was talking fast now.

"All right! So why didn't yuh wait for her?" Grapes thundered. "Aim t' let her walk?"

Harve read the swift breakdown of his story if he did not bolster it up. "Why, uh—I noticed some hombres watchin' me right close, there in Dutch Springs. An' sure enough, somebody followed when I pulled away. Dang it, Ern, with that rig I couldn't take to the open range; I *had* to keep movin'! What would you've done?" he demanded fiercely.

Ernie proceeded to tell him. The talk became a pointless wrangle; and beyond noticing that MacEwen was following every word with painful care, Pat lost interest. Wells finally managed to brush Grapes off, and demanded some food. He disappeared into the house with Doc, and Ernie prowled about restlessly like a cat on hot bricks. Later Pat observed Grapes and young MacEwen deep in guarded talk in a corner of the yard. They were arguing about something, and Ernie appeared to be blaming Brad.

They were still at it when Wells emerged on the porch. The sun was sinking toward the horizon and he stood briefly gazing at it, his eyes shaded, taking no notice of the pair beyond a gruff exclamation for Grapes's benefit.

"Said yuh was makin' a stew about nothing, didn't I?" His voice sounded exultant. "She's comin' now, Ern—"

The others whirled. Through the golden haze of sunset they made out a slowly approaching figure. It was Letty. MacEwen ran out to grasp her bridle as she wearily dismounted.

"Are you plumb crazy?" he hissed under his breath. "You got clear away. Why didn't you stay away?"

She only looked at him wordlessly.

Ernie came walking forward, on the warpath from his looks. "Where'd yuh get that horse?" he thundered. "Yuh rode out o' here in the rig—"

She looked surprised. "Why, we're known in Dutch Springs, Dad." Her explanation was chiding. "I borrowed it from Mr. Winters at the store—"

"Well, we'll get it back there then." He was stern. "That's one thing I won't have against me or mine!"

Stepping out of the door at that moment, Pat caught the concluding words clearly. He glanced quickly at Wells. If any of this bunch should be asking themselves about the state of Ernie Grapes's morals, this remark was answer in full. The old rawhide was as firmly sold on honesty as on the day, years ago, when he had promised Gif Towner he would go straight. But Harve, grinning at the other's vehemence, appeared to notice nothing.

The outlaw escorted Letty into the cluttered house, making a fuss over her. If anything it was overdone. Watching the girl critically, Pat thought she looked literally fed up, and at the same time shrinkingly wary of Wells.

Doc and Chet Denton watched the proceedings uneasily. It was perfectly obvious that a spirit of deep and growing unrest weighed on everyone except Harve himself; yet the preoccupied leader successfully ignored it. He appeared to possess some secret he was trying to hide, yet which buoyed up his spirits.

Once more Denton threw a sketchy meal together, Pat volunteering his aid. The girl had retired upstairs. Waiting in the big room, Wells attempted to joke and prod Grapes into speech. Ernie refused to commit himself. Dour and restless, he appeared on the point of an explosion.

He held off; and calling Letty to join them, they sat down to supper. It proved an awkward meal, Doc and Denton shooting repeated furtive glances at the girl. They resented her return, chiefly because it would render Wells more stubborn than ever to deal with. Harve himself was expansive.

"You boys are just huntin' trouble," he observed, smiling at the somber faces. "We're all together, ain't we—and everything's jake."

"Wonder if Gila's feelin' that way," remarked Doc idly.

Wells waved a hand. "Cut it out, Doc. Gila was gettin' too big for his pants. The way Stevens is shapin' up, he ought to be able to fill Gila's boots."

There was a double meaning in the words that brought momentary silence. If Pat got it he failed to react, however. He knew Harve felt that he now held a powerful hold on him, and perhaps even intended to play Gila's friends off against him when the moment arose.

Old Ernie's silence effectively hid his thoughts; but it was proven presently that he had missed nothing. Letty's departure to return to her room seemed the signal for which her father had been waiting.

"What now, Wells?" Denton demanded as they shoved their empty plates back. "Are we waitin' here for Towner to show up—or what?"

"You're fools if yuh do," Grapes suddenly interrupted. "Stevens is dead right, boys! Either we're all in this together, or we ain't. We all got a right to our say—an' I say things look plumb bad . . . I don't care what yuh plan about gettin' together later," he continued. "Right now I move we split the haul—any way yuh think's fair'll do me—an' drift. This bird," he gestured fiercely toward Wells, "is crossin' us all! Trot that money out, Wells," he challenged flatly. "We'll get this over with pronto!"

Harve waited only to see the resolute nods of agreement

that ran around the circle. Then he began to chuckle and burst finally into a roar of laughter.

"You're too late, Ern," he managed to say. "The boys thought it was queer I insisted on takin' Letty to town. I can tell yuh why now . . . She took that money to the Dutch Springs bank and deposited it all—in her name!"

Once more he broke into a hearty guffaw, firmly assured he had played an excellent joke on them all, particularly on Grapes.

Doc and Chet Denton exploded in angry recriminations, and old Ernie towered with rage.

"Yuh aim to spend it all with her too, I reckon," he thundered. "You're a smooth article, Wells! This time yuh went too far. Think yuh got a grip on me now I can't break, do yuh!" Blazing with indignation, he stood up, knocking his chair down, and stalked from the room.

Hot words followed, but Pat realized the finality of the situation. Wells had indeed lit a smoldering fuse that could never be put out. Suspicion, jealousy, greed gnawed this gang and it could be only a matter of time before the explosion. The others felt it. They made no secret of their split with Wells, and just as clearly they expected Ernie Grapes to make the first move.

Would it be gun play? Doc's waiting calm said that he hoped as much. Ernie Grapes's reputation had once been formidable. Harve saw their naked enmity, and attempted to bluff it out.

"I'm hittin' the hay," he announced, with exaggerated coolness. "By mornin', if you're cooled off, I'll talk to yuh." He brazenly turned his back on them.

Pat would have given something for a talk tonight with Ezra and Sam. But Denton took over the watch, and Stevens moved out into the open to bed down behind the corral where dried and brittle tumbleweed would give ample warning of prowlers during the dark hours.

The place settled into ominous silence, and Pat slept better than he had expected. He was awakened at dawn by a bawl of rage from the direction of the house. He started up, blinking. Harve Wells stood in the kitchen door, brandishing his arms and raving wildly.

Yanking his boots on, Pat ran forward. "What's wrong?" he yelled.

"Plenty, Stevens! It's that devil Grapes!" Wells choked with fury. "He's gone! They're both gone—"

"*Both?*" Pat barked.

"Him and Letty! They must've sneaked out durin' the night," gasped Harve. "They've run out on me!"

Stark disbelief rang in the words, but Pat understood in a flash. Although he had previously nursed an undying grudge against Wells, Letty's father had been stung to frenzy by the outlaw's cold, calculating treachery. This was Grapes's answer.

14.

Doc CAME THUMPING and clattering down the stairs, having satisfied himself that all trace of the girl was gone. His face was thunderous.

"This is your doin', Wells," he broke in harshly. "Yuh think you're so dang cute! There ain't nothin' to be gained by blowin' about old Ernie. Seemed smart to stall us when we wanted our cut, didn't it? I hope to thunder you never see your own!"

"I'll see it, all right! Don't sweat yourself about that," the outlaw fumed.

"Just how'll yuh do it?" asked Brad MacEwen, contemptuously. He alone seemed visibly cheered by Letty's departure, and it made him bold. "Seems to me that you're in Gila's fix, Wells. You asked for this. How do yuh like it?"

Not even Harve could deny that his authority with this hard-bitten bunch had slipped badly overnight, but it was second nature for him to pretend to ignore the fact.

"I don't follow yuh, kid. Just how did I ask for it?" he snapped.

"It's you who dragged a girl into this rotten business," accused Brad flatly. "Don't say you didn't know none of us liked the idea! We argued with yuh. But no—it was goin' to put Ernie Grapes on our side, accordin' to you. Yuh see now how it worked!"

"You're dead right, Mac," Doc seconded. "Chuck it into him good an' hard—"

"I'll bale it at him," rasped Brad resolutely. "I've been savin' this. We all have, and what's more he knows it!"

"Heave ahead, MacEwen." Wells sneered. "Get it out of your system while you're able!"

"You let us think that once we dragged Ernie well into the game, he'd send Letty packin' off home," Brad charged heatedly. "Everything'd be fine then—you said . . . You was sure all the time it was on your precious account that Letty was here, and down in your rotten heart you wanted it that way!"

Pat had been following keenly every twist and turn of the quarrel. He coolly calculated its ultimate effect on Wells, and decided to give it a push in the right direction.

"Hold on there, Mac," he said mildly. "Let's not make Harve out any blacker than he is."

Brad shot him a look. "Huh—?"

"You're the handsome hombre that Letty Grapes followed this far," Pat told him levelly. "You know it and I know it. Hasn't she tried over and over to get you to give this life up? . . . Oh, I know how it looked," he continued blandly. "Nobody blames the girl for not wantin' Wells to catch on. Old Ernie himself was plumb surprised when I tipped him off!"

Harve absorbed the startling words with painful incredulity. If Letty had not left so suddenly, he wouldn't have believed it for a second. Now, however, he paused, and suspicion flamed through him.

"What's all this?" He threw the weight of his anger against Pat. "Up to your old tricks again, Stevens? Tryin' hard to start somethin', ain't yuh!"

"I don't reckon he is," drawled Doc. "Anybody but you would've seen it comin', Harve. Ever stop to think of her age—and then your own? Yuh come back from Dutch Springs with a pretty yarn about havin' to run, but we all know well enough the girl ditched yuh. It wasn't you that brought her draggin' back here, neither—"

"And I can tell you something else," Brad whipped out, confronting Wells squarely. "Letty's gone. *Don't make the mistake of tryin' to find her*. Or it'll be your finish, Wells!"

But for Pat's presence, Harve would have gunned Brad down without hesitation. But the outlaw realized his danger. Relentless pressure was being exerted by every member of this gang. He knew only one way to meet such a combination.

"It'll be my finish if I don't!" he exclaimed harshly. "Grapes may think he'll spend that money—or maybe *you* do, MacEwen. But I'm going to prove how wrong yuh can be!"

"I'll go along with yuh there, Harve," inserted Doc. "It concerns me what becomes of that haul. You lost it. You'll get it back, or answer for it." He issued his ultimatum. "How do yuh propose to go about it?"

The bluntness of this gave them all pause. Pat was the first to speak.

"Just a second," he said quickly. "You're none of you bashful about givin' orders. Seems to me Chet Denton's got a right to his word here. Where is Chet?"

"Harve chased him off to Canyon, Stevens, soon as we found Grapes and the girl gone." Doc's answer was offhand. "Yuh don't think we'd let them slope without tryin' to stop 'em, do yuh?"

Pat moved quickly to the door and peered up the trail.

"Somebody comin' now," he announced tensely. "Pushin' his bronc hard, too . . . By gravy, it's Denton, all right. And he's alone!"

They hurried outside to look. What Pat said was true. Chet Denton was racing toward them as if the devil were after him. He rode close, and hauled in with a scatter of gravel.

"What about it, Chet?" Wells demanded. "Did they go that way—or didn't they?"

Denton's crooked smile was hard and humorless. "I wouldn't know. Never caught up with 'em, boys. But I did almost fall over Gif Towner." He told the startling news calmly. "Figured yuh'd like to know—"

"Towner, yuh say?" Wells tightened up in a flash. "Where'd yuh run into him, Dent?"

"Gif's prowlin' around Canyon." Chet was terse. "I reckon he expected to corner us there. He'll find out his mistake—an' it's only a matter of time before he shows up here."

"So he'll show up." Doc was laconic. "Blast his hide, we'll soon make him turn tail—!"

"Not this time, yuh won't." Chet grinned fleetingly. "I didn't wait to count his posse, but there's eight or ten anyhow."

The silence was tense as they digested this news. Wells rose to the emergency with his usual arrogance.

"We ain't married to this shack," he said harshly. "Get your traps together, boys. We'll lose that bunch like water off a duck's back. Jump now!"

Pat was one of the first to be ready to ride. "Take a turn down the trail, Stevens," Harve ordered, hurriedly lashing a pack. "Won't do no harm to keep an eye peeled."

"What about those hombres you're holdin' inside?" asked Pat, gesturing in Sam and Ezra's direction. "We leavin' them here, I expect?"

"Hell no." Harve's laugh rang hard. "We might use 'em later as bait. If Towner thinks he's got it in for me, maybe we can hand him a surprise."

Pat jogged down the trail, mulling this over. But for MacEwen and the partners, it might be possible to delay the gang long enough to enable the federal marshal to grab them all. Stevens, however, was taking no chances. A quarter mile from the house he drew rein abruptly. Far off in the direction of Canyon he spotted a string of tiny figures filing through a gap. They were working this way, and there could be little doubt as to their identity.

Wells and the others were gathered in the yard when Pat raced back.

"Bad news, eh, Stevens?"

He nodded. "Towner's less than a mile away, and coming steady."

They were ready. Denton finished binding Ez and Sam's hands and lashing them in the saddle. He swung astride. "Anything holdin' us back?"

Crossing the gravelly bench, directly away from the trail, they filed into a rock-walled canyon winding into the hills. They pushed on steadily, and nothing was said. For a time Wells rode in the rear, looking back with narrow attention. An hour put considerable distance behind them; but as the sun rose higher the deceptive morning shadows faded, cutting their protection to a minimum, and they lost no time.

Pat saw to it that he rode near the gloomy captives. Although they made no other attempt at communication, their scowling, faintly accusing glances rested on him from time to time. Pat was content with the assurance that they were in no particular danger.

By midmorning they reached a higher level and passed into the pines. They were on the northern slope of the Culebras now, an area incredibly wild, broken and remote. More than once elk crashed away from them through the balsam scrub, and they came across the remains of a cougar-killed deer. Any man knowing this country well, as Pat did, could have saved weary miles of travel and shaken off the posse in short order. Yet he held his tongue.

Later, as they filed through solemn fir parks and climbed the craggy passes, Stevens found himself riding near Brad MacEwen. The young fellow had something on his mind, but he waited to speak till they were somewhat separated from the others.

"What was the big idea of throwin' it in Harve's teeth about Letty and me, Stevens?" he began in a tone that was far from friendly.

Pat's glance was amused. "Oh, that? Reckon I thought it might slow him up a bit—"

"Slow him up!" Brad was bitter. "He'll want to tear Letty apart now, and you know it!"

"That's about where you come in, ain't it?" retorted Pat calmly. "What are you stickin' with us for, anyway? I expected you to pull out the minute you knew Letty and her father were safe."

Brad struggled with himself briefly. It was plain that Pat had touched a sensitive spot. "I'll beat Wells to old Ernie's ranch, whatever happens," he declared darkly. This was an evasion, and Pat knew it.

"What *is* Harve's hold on you, MacEwen?" he demanded bluntly.

"Nothin'. Not a thing in this world!" Brad was fervent. "But what ever yuh may think, Stevens, you simply don't know him like I do—"

"Don't tell me he fascinates you!" Pat's tone was ironic. It succeeded in arousing MacEwen to a fresh show of resentment.

"Dammit, man! You know what he is," he burst out. "Close kin to a rattlesnake, only more treacherous! All that talk about wantin' Ernie Grapes in the gang . . . It may be news to you that Harve hates Grapes like poison. He's sworn to smash Ernie—land him in the pen for life; and Letty's just a part of his game! Do you get it now?''

Pat sobered swiftly. "You mean you've set yourself to watch Wells?'' he murmured softly. "You're not riding with this crowd because you like it and want it that way?''

MacEwen's eyes flashed. *"Like it?* This bunch? . . . I told you the answer to that before, Stevens! I'd see them in hell in a minute, if I could work it!''

Pat's nod was measured. "Would you go back to punchin' cows if Wells was out of the way?'' he probed.

Brad's look betrayed him before he could speak. "Just give me the chance!'' he breathed.

They broke off as Doc halted in the trail to look back at them. Prodding their horses, they shoved on. Not long after this they found Harve and the others hauled up in a rocky hollow almost completely masked by gnarled cedar.

"We'll risk stoppin' long enough to make coffee,'' the cold-faced leader announced. "If Towner makes me miss breakfast another time, I'll know all about it!''

Doc started a small fire while Denton opened the food pack. They waited impatiently for the fragrant coffee to come to a boil.

"What was you an' Stevens jawin' about back there?'' Harve said unexpectedly to MacEwen.

Brad met him head-on. "You,'' he snapped.

"Hope yuh got somewheres.'' Wells nodded as if he had expected nothing better. "Your time is comin', MacEwen—''

Doc's lips curled at the bluster in this vague threat. "Lay off the bickerin', for Lord sake,'' he growled wearily. "Blamed if I ain't gettin' a bellyful of yuh both—''

Denton, saying nothing, took time to climb the rocks and gaze over their back trail. He had barely reached the top when a leaden slug screamed suddenly off a granite face and lashed through the cedar branches. A shower of clipped needles sifted down on the startled group below. A split-second later they heard the delayed spang of the rifle.

Wells sprang erect with a howl of dismay. "What the hell! That can't be Towner on our heels?'' he cried piercingly.

Chet came tumbling down the rocks and ran swiftly for

his horse. "Stay an' find out, if yuh want," he rasped. "I'm travelin'!"

Coffee forgotten, they took to their mounts in scrambling disorder. Harve led, and the rest tumbled after as best they could.

"What are you up to?" thundered Pat, as Doc surreptitiously drew his gun. Doc looked surprised and annoyed.

"No need of them two taggin' along any further." He jerked his chin toward Sam and Ez. "Let Towner scratch his head over their carcasses, Stevens, while we're makin' time away from here—"

Pat turned his horse into the other's and blocked the cold-blooded play. "On your way, you. I don't aim to swing for your crazy foolishness!"

The command was not to be denied. Doc whirled his horse with an oath and crashed on. After that Pat saw to it that he stayed between the owlhoot and their captives, although Doc did not even look at them again. Indeed, none of them found time for private troubles. More than once as the afternoon ran on, high-powered rifles cracked spitefully to the rear, and the ominous whine of bullets lent the fugitives added speed.

Not till late afternoon, with the gloomy grandeur of the ragged mountains hemming them in on all sides, the sun low in the west, did it begin to appear that they had at last shaken off pursuit temporarily. At dusk Wells turned into a secluded canyon pocket, where he dismounted wearily.

"What are yuh aimin' to do?" Doc snapped.

"I'm stoppin' to rest if I have to fight off Custer's army," Harve retorted. "We'll be safe here till mornin'—"

"Yuh can do as you're a mind to." Doc was equally deadly. "I'm shovin' on. And I ain't stoppin' short of the Isabels—or mebby the Utah line!"

"That goes for me too," put in Denton abruptly. He tried to argue Wells into pushing on, but Harve waved a hand decisively.

"No dice, boys. I'm here, and here I stop."

Doc started to turn away, only to halt. "About that money of ours, Harve," he murmured with chilling smoothness. "Better get it back, and fast! . . . We'll be waitin' for yuh, say at Brown's Park. Yuh got a month to make

good. After that,'' he added casually, ''we'll come lookin'
for yuh!''

Wells nodded stonily. This was their parting. After
riding with him for weeks, Doc and Chet Denton turned
their ponies and trotted off without a backward glance.

As the sound of their departure died away, Harve tried
to sneer it off, and glared at Pat and MacEwen. ''Stayin'
with me, are yuh?'' he growled. ''Yuh may turn out to be
safer company than those fools, at that!''

''We're still here, Wells.'' Pat's response was cool.
''Did you figure you could maybe get rid of us too?''

Offering his gaunted horse a hatful of feed, Wells pretended to find no special significance in the remark. But he
whipped to attention a moment later as Pat started to strip
the bonds from Ezra and Sam.

''Hold on, there! What are yuh doin' with that pair?'' he
ripped out in alarm.

''No point in hidin' it any longer,'' Pat told him flatly.
''These two happen to be good friends of mine, Wells.
Maybe the four of us can manage to turn you over to Gif
Towner without any further trouble—''

MacEwen saw the outlaw's hand steal toward his bridle,
and started to whip his gun out. Wells shot it out of his
hand. With Pat at a momentary disadvantage, the menacing muzzle of his weapon covering them all, Harve crawled
into the saddle, a snarl contorting his face.

''Hold it, all of yuh!'' he ground out in a drone. ''I seen
this comin'! It's my turn to pull out now. But I'll come
back, MacEwen; and I'll get you if it's the last thing I
do—after I square accounts with that double-crossin' dame!''

15.

A SCRAPE OF HOOFS died out on naked rock and Harve Wells was gone.

"Cripes!" breathed Pat as their tension began to relax. "To think that buzzard would have to look like me—"

"Hustle it up, Stevens!" Ezra interrupted, struggling with his loosened bonds. "Get these ropes off, an' we may have a chance t' grab that slob before he gets away!"

Pat thought this over briefly, and regretfully shook his head. "Our broncs are exhausted, boys, and Wells has all the advantage. No use breakin' our hearts. We'll let him come to us."

Sam glanced up keenly. "How do yuh figure that?" he demanded.

"You heard him. He won't be able to leave that girl alone," Pat pointed out coolly. "When he comes after her, we'll be waitin'."

MacEwen was gloomily wrapping a deep scratch on his hand with a kerchief. His fingers were numb after having the gun shot out of his grip, but he had escaped without worse injury.

"It's my fault," he muttered glumly. "I should've shot him down days ago, from behind or any other way, like the wolf he is. Somehow I couldn't do it—"

Pat clapped him on the shoulder. "Let it ride, boy. We're all at a disadvantage in dealing with his kind. Something like this was bound to happen—and you've still got Letty to think about."

"Seems t' me yuh didn't have much trouble dealin' with Gila," growled Sam, kicking the last of his bonds off his legs. "Pity it wasn't Wells—"

Pat laughed. "Gila was the mad-dog kind, never to be

122

trusted a minute. He made up his mind long ago to pick a quarrel with me. It was him or me—and I picked my own time for the showdown.''

Twilight cast a gray veil over the forest as they talked. It would be night in a matter of minutes, but that meant little to young Brad. "Better take off for the Circle G, hadn't we?" He was prowling restlessly back and forth. "If Harve beats us there, I'll never forgive myself!"

"Slack off, will yuh?" Ez was gruff. "Wells has got his own headaches right now—Gif Towner amongst 'em . . . Like it or not, we're stayin' right here till mornin'."

Pat assented. "It's only common sense, MacEwen."

They lighted a fire and made camp. Although they were ravenous, there was no hope of downing game in the gathering darkness, and their supplies had been abandoned during the flight from the marshal's posse. There was only a little coffee Sloan had been carrying in a saddlebag, and, after sipping this, they tightened their belts and rolled in their blankets after making sure the ponies had plenty of browse.

At this altitude, in mid-October, it grew bitter cold toward morning. Pat built up the fire a couple of times, and he was glad to get on his feet with the first streaks of light the following morning. The others were not far behind him.

They shared the little coffee that was left, and Sam and Ez at least were reluctant to leave the fire.

"Yuh pickin' up Towner's posse on the way down, Stevens?" the redhead asked as he saddled up.

Pat had been thinking about it. But there was little information they could offer the federal lawman, now that Wells's gang had scattered.

"I think we'll let well enough alone," he decided. "Gif could ask MacEwen here some mighty embarrassin' questions. And if we aim to play our own hand there at Ernie's place, Towner would never consent. He thinks he's been burned once already."

"Well, are we gettin' down there or not?" Brad was feverishly impatient. "Let's go, Stevens! I won't be satisfied till I know Letty's all right."

They set off, angling down the long slopes and climbing

the intervening ridges. It was a long hard ride, circling down timber and heading the gorgelike canyons. Toward midday Sam downed a doe just as they came out on the eastern slope of the Culebras, though it was hard for MacEwen to haul up long enough to broil some of the tender meat.

Having eaten, they shoved on in better spirits. There had been no sign of Towner's posse. In fact, for hours they had come across no evidence whatever of any human activities. But in early afternoon, gazing down a long slant, Ezra pointed out what he said was Grapes's ranch house. An hour later they approached the place cautiously, looking it over with care. MacEwen was the first to detect the marks of occupancy.

"That's Letty's pony in the corral," he exclaimed. "She must be in the house—and Ernie can't be far away, either."

They spied Grapes a moment later, moving across the yard, rifle in hand. He stiffened at sight of them, and started for the corner of the house, but relaxed when MacEwen called out.

Waiting, Grapes scrutinized them shrewdly from under shaggy brows. He noted the absence of bonds on Ezra and Sam, and gave Pat a significant look. "I see you're alone," was his crusty comment. "I trust nothin' serious happened t' Wells—"

"We had to run when Towner showed up with a posse," explained Pat. "Harve and the others finally pulled away from us."

Brad put in a word, and Grapes was soon acquainted with events following his own departure. The kitchen screen slammed and Letty appeared. Her face lit up as MacEwen slid from the saddle and moved that way. There were smiles on both their faces as they met, the girl's eyes expressing wonder and doubt.

"You've—come back, Brad?"

Conscious of an audience, he tried to nod casually. "I'll be around a while, if yuh don't mind—"

"Mind!" She seemed scarcely able to tear her gaze away from him. "But I . . . don't understand." She broke off nervously. "Where is—is—"

"Harve Wells, yuh mean?" he supplied gruffly. "We think he'll be back, Letty, I'm sorry to say."

"Oh!" Abruptly she understood. "On my account, you mean. It's my fault, of course. But—" She blanched. "You'll be waiting for him. Is that it?"

Pat thought it time to intervene, and stepped forward calmly. "Hope you don't mind being used for bait, Letty." He smiled apologetically. "It's our only chance now—and we'll try to make sure that wolf never gets to you. That's if he shows up at all," he qualified easily.

Letty was under few illusions on that score. "I'm sure he will come," she half-whispered. And then, more strongly: "Whatever possessed me to touch that money? It—seemed such a wonderful idea at the time! . . . But almost at once I realized Mr. Wells would never let it go like this—that he would insist I must return his—the—money."

"It's in your name, then?" Ez probed.

"He suggested a joint account. I told him I meant to put it in my name alone—and I did."

"What happened after?"

"I'm afraid I—slipped away and hid." She flushed. "I could stand no more of that man."

Brad's face showed how much the answer meant to him. He was unable to leave it at that. "Yuh come back, though."

The girl's cheeks were rosy now. "I suppose I was thinking of Father," she murmured. The young fellow's obvious chagrin indicated that the remark had hit home.

"Shucks, ain't we never goin' t' eat?" Ez muttered to Pat, loudly enough to be heard. Letty started, and then she rushed toward the house.

"What am I thinking of?" she exclaimed. "Wash up, all of you! I'll have food at the table before you're—"

It was an animated meal, with considerable talk after the first pangs of hunger were satisfied. Pat made opportunity to speak to MacEwen in private, soon after the dishes were cleared away.

"You must know, Brad, that sooner or later Gif Towner is bound to show up here," he began.

MacEwen's brows knit. "I know it. He's probably got me lined up as one of that gang—"

"After all, you were in that bank." Pat nodded, extending no false hope. "I'm just warning you beforehand—"

Brad had already been thinking it over. "I plan to lay out in the hills, Stevens, close enough to spot Wells in time," he said. "Letty will bring me grub."

"No, no." Pat was firm. "She *should* be in town till this is over, but I don't suppose she'd consent. We'll be around though, and we can take good care of you."

Agreeing on details, they presently parted. Soon afterward, swinging astride his pony, MacEwen reluctantly jogged away. The craggy cliff overlooking the ranch was an ideal point from which to maintain a watch; and it was from there that Brad would keep an eye open for Pat's signals.

With the young fellow's departure, affairs appeared to settle into a routine. Expecting Wells's arrival at any time, and ready for it, old Ernie would not have left the place at all had not Stevens persuaded him to carry on the ranch work as usual. For safety's sake the men traveled in pairs, and at no time was the ranch left wholly unguarded.

An uneasy day passed, and another. All were beginning to feel the strain as time ran on and Harve did not appear. Perhaps the outlaw counted on this effect—unless he was still running and hiding from Towner's posse. Pat never forgot, however, that Doc and Chet Denton had given the cocky leader a deadline for recovering the stolen money. Sooner or later the pressure must build up on Wells and he would come prowling slyly, watching his chance to pounce on the girl.

On the third morning Letty was serving up breakfast in the kitchen when a sudden bang made them all jump.

"What was that?" Sam exclaimed.

None knew. It seemed to have come from overhead, however. They were discussing it when again the sharp crack sounded, to be followed by a bouncing dribble. Pat held up his hand, realizing what was happening.

"It's rocks, tossed on the roof," he announced briefly. "MacEwen is trying to warn us from the cliff."

They stiffened, and Letty dropped a fork she had been holding. "Then that means—"

Stevens shrugged. "Either Brad's spotted Wells on his

way here, or . . .'' He did not continue, swinging his cartridge belt around his hips and buckling it.

Scooping up a rifle, old Ernie sprang to the window with remarkable agility. He froze, and they heard a grunt as he slowly straightened up.

'' 'Tain't Harve,'' he told them, his tone dull. Ezra reached the rancher's side and had his own look.

"Why, that's Gif Towner comin','' he said gruffly. "He's all alone. What can he be wantin' here?''

As she moved quickly to old Ernie's side, Letty unconsciously betrayed her own fears. "Never mind, Dad,'' she encouraged quietly. "There's nothing he can honestly accuse you of—''

Grapes growled, pushed her away and started grimly for the door. Pat and the partners followed. They waited outside as Marshal Towner jogged slowly forward.

He looked over the four men, and saw Letty standing in the door. "Lookin' for me, was yuh?'' he asked woodenly, his lips tight.

Grapes's nod was stiff. "Had an idea yuh'd be around—''

Towner dismounted unhurriedly. "Maybe yuh'd like to step over here a ways for a word alone, Ern,'' he suggested coolly.

Pat spoke up as the rancher hesitated. "I take it you haven't caught up with Wells, Towner,'' he ventured.

Gif was disgusted. "Thought you was aimin' to arrange that,'' he retorted. He scrutinized the ranch. "Harve wouldn't be around now, by any chance—?''

Although he'd been about to grant Gif an interview, old Ernie balked at this, his leathery face set. "Don't be gettin' smart, Towner,'' he bawled heatedly. "The only way that rat'd be hangin' around here is dead!'' He glared his challenge, breathing heavily. "Since yuh feel that way, say what yuh got t' say, an' we'll get this over with!''

Briefly taken aback, the lawman finally got a grip on himself. "I come here, Grapes,'' he remarked dryly, "to hear what *you* got to say.'' He paused. "Out with it! What do yuh know about Harve Wells?''

"Nothin','' the rancher fired back promptly. Gif shook his head gravely.

"It won't do, Ern.'' The words were final. "Yuh was

found in his camp—and I *know* yuh been ridin' with him. Your refusal to talk amounts to aidin' and abettin' criminal activities!"

"Thought yuh'd take that slant!" Grapes's grim face closed. "Well, Harve pulled away from us two days ago, somewheres in the Culebras. I dunno where he is."

"Don't give me that." Towner seemed mystified and angered. "Yuh must know somethin'! Hell, man, I've been givin' yuh all the breaks. Just don't try to make a sucker out of me—"

"Tell yuh I don't know no more," roared Ernie. "Can't yuh understand English?"

"Slack off, Grapes," advised Pat, speaking up for the first time. "If I guess right, Towner thinks yuh got some cross-grained notion in your head about not givin' the gang away, no matter what happens."

But Ernie was not to be stopped now. "Give it away?" he echoed contemptuously. "Yuh can have the kit an' kaboodle, Towner, an' welcome!"

Gif knew blind stubbornness when he saw it, but he had his own brand of persistence. He shook his head dourly. "Are yuh talkin', old man, or not?"

All saw by his deliberate manner that he was on the verge of a decision. Letty appeared to guess accurately what it must be, for once more she advanced to her father's side.

"You've no right to crowd Dad this way, Marshal," she declared boldly. "Especially after he has told you what little he does know—"

Gif scowled his plain distaste for being browbeaten. "Sure of that, are yuh!"

The girl's voice rose clear and sharp. "Yes, Mr. Towner. I am!"

"Easy, girl, easy." Gif glowered. "I'll just remind yuh that you're under a shadow yourself. Yuh were not only in Antler, but yuh were seen right in the bank itself, when it was robbed—"

"Blast it, Towner! Marshal or no marshal, that does it!" Old Ernie's jowls corded, his face darkening. "Yuh can think what yuh damned please, but yuh ain't got a thing on either of us. Unless you're prepared t' act on suspicion—and make it stick—I'll ask yuh to get off this ranch an' stay off it!''

That got to the lawman. Although he began to fume, it was clear that he found nothing pertinent to say. Nor, apparently, could he bring himself to follow the perilous course Grapes suggested. Under the latter's steady glare, he shifted from one leg to the other and finally turned to leave.

"Right now, as it happens, I got other business," he allowed gruffly. "The time is comin', Grapes, when I'll be lookin' real close into your case. And when I do, yuh'll see me again!''

Silence hung as he mounted his horse and turned away. Watching him go, Ezra began to chuckle. Sloan, however, found nothing humorous in the moment.

"That could turn out t' be a mistake, Stevens, sendin' Towner packin' that way,'' exclaimed Sam earnestly. "Yuh heard what he said!''

Pat shrugged. "It's done now. Personally I'd prefer to turn Wells over to him, along with that money in the Dutch Springs bank. Any other way, Sam, he could never be dead sure we didn't simply scare out.''

Grapes nodded curtly. "I thought yuh'd get it.''

They got it all right. But Sam could not forget the federal marshal's veiled threat. "I still think it was a mistake,'' he insisted soberly.

To what extent he was right was to be demonstrated within another twelve hours. Twenty minutes after Towner disappeared on the trail to town, MacEwen rode in, curious to know what had been going on. Pat let him have half an hour with Letty before he broke it up. A mention of Harve Wells was enough. Almost guiltily Brad returned to his lookout, and the others scattered to various parts of the range.

The day passed, and Pat was returning at suppertime when he saw Ezra coming forward accompanied by a stranger. He called Grapes, and together they waited at the edge of the yard.

"Huh!'' Ernie's grunt was colorless. "Thought so!''

The newcomer with Ez was Poke Donner, recently elected sheriff of Powder County.

"Here yuh are, Grapes," he greeted sourly, hauling up. "Saves trouble huntin' for yuh anyhow . . . Get up a bronc, will yuh? I'm takin' yuh in—"

Ernie knew what this meant. He stared, reddening. "Takin' me in! What for?"

Donner stolidly pulled out a paper. "Rustlin', it says here. Rafe Alford's Rafter A stuff, if you've forgot already . . . Tracks was traced this way a week ago—an' finally we found a Rafter A cow, overbranded Tomahawk, on your lower range." He shook his head dolefully. "Too bad, Ern. Reckon there can't be no mistake about it!"

Pat stared fixedly at the sheriff. He understood. This was the next move in Gif Towner's devious game, and for the moment it bore all the earmarks of a knockout.

16.

GRAPES GAVE THE LAWMAN a withering glare. "What's too bad, Donner—that you're runnin' another man's errand for him? Next yuh'll be tellin' me you're sorry about this—"

Poke swallowed hard several times. "Yuh ain't gettin' nowheres, talkin' that way!" he choked, his large jaw working.

"Ain't figurin' t' go nowheres." Ernie chuckled contemptuously. "With you, or without you!"

Donner looked as if he had never enjoyed life, and certainly did not expect to henceforth. His face was long and doleful. His pale eyes bulged somewhat, and gave him a truculent air.

"Well, now—yuh know yourself rustlin's somethin' that can't be overlooked," he argued. "Alford's been givin' me a hard time. No use blamin' me, Ernie. I've held off long as I got a right to—"

"Hold off a while longer, then," retorted the rancher sharply. "I sent Towner packin' outa here—an' it won't be no different with you!"

Donner had been thinking fast since seeing the old rawhide's temper. He may have expected to find Ernie alone; but Pat's presence had already put a strain on his authority—and out of the corner of his eye Poke noticed Ezra and Sam, unsaddling at the corral. Knowing the trio of old, he was clearly dubious about pushing his luck.

Pat saw his eyes waver. "No need to be in a hurry about this, Donner," he suggested reasonably. "Have you talked to Towner?"

Poke declined to take the bait. "Right now I'm on business of my own—"

"Yes, but you know yourself it's almost impossible to

131

get a conviction for rustling,'' Pat drove on flatly. ''You found an overbranded steer. So the rustlers lost a stray, crossin' a corner of Grapes's range! If that's the evidence you hand a jury, Sheriff, the commissioners will be takin' you aside for a little talk . . . Trials cost the county just as much money,'' he reminded him shrewdly, ''when the verdict turns out to be 'not guilty.' ''

It was only common sense, and Donner had not paused to look at matters in that light before. He scratched his jaw dourly. ''Well, I dunno.'' He had no intention of giving up easily. ''Ernie's record is plumb against him, Stevens. Yuh won't deny that. Who's t' say a jury of smart cowmen'll swallow his yarn about bein' took advantage of—if that *is* his defense?''

''You an' your 'defense,' '' snorted Grapes fiercely. ''Just try haulin' me up, Donner, an' so help me,'' he swore, ''if I beat the case I'll make life a misery for you, and don't yuh forget it!''

Poke did not find this second reminder of the possible outcome any easier to take than the first. He began to get mean.

''Blast it, Grapes! Where'll I wind up if the voters hear I can't be bothered t' push this case? Worse'n that—the lightfingered hombres'll be movin' in on us in droves!''

''That,'' Pat told him levelly, ''is your headache. You've been warned, Donner, of what you're up against. I'll make it my business to back Ernie to the hilt. Now. Will you push this ridiculous charge—or shall I ride to Dutch Springs with you and we'll go over the business sensibly with Gif Towner?''

Jealous of his rights, Poke regarded the proposal with cold suspicion. ''What's he got to do with it?''

''He's got federal authority. Could be he knows more about this rustling than he lets on,'' remarked Pat shrewdly. ''Good grief, Sheriff! What's your rush? Grapes told you he's not going anywheres. A rancher, I might add, with an investment a whole lot bigger than yours. You'll be able to find him right here, any time you want.''

Donner was impressed. ''Yuh say you aim to talk to Towner yourself?''

''It's about time somebody did.'' Pat was firm. ''Wait

till I get up a bronc. I'll go back with you right now, and maybe we can square this foolishness without any more loss of time."

He did not wait for Donner's half-hearted reply, making for the corral to get a mount. Poke was still hammering at Ernie when he got back.

"—want yuh to consider yourself at my disposal," the lawman was insisting dogmatically. "Just see that you're handy when I want yuh, Grapes, an' don't be takin' no long trips!"

Ernie snorted. To a man on parole for years, this was idle talk. The rancher disdained to answer and watched Pat and the sheriff jog away in the direction of town.

Pat occupied himself during the long ride by trying to learn just how concrete was Donner's rustling evidence against Grapes. He put question after question, and was not much surprised when the lawman persistently evaded. In time Pat became certain that his original suspicion was correct. He nodded to himself. "Towner and I will sure have somethin' to talk about," he reflected grimly.

It was after dark when they reached Dutch Springs. Far more townspeople called greetings to Stevens than took any notice whatever of the sheriff, and noting this, Poke was much annoyed. Pat appeared not to notice. "I suppose Gif's at the hotel?" he remarked.

"Was," Donner assented unguardedly. It was a further proof that the law enforcement officers had already talked together about Ernie Grapes.

They were nearing the hotel when a man came out of the Gold Eagle to accost Poke. After a brief exchange, Donner turned back to Pat disgustedly.

"I'll be busy for half an hour, Stevens," he growled. "Yuh waitin' for me, or not?"

"I'll look Towner up while I'm here," returned Pat, pleased to be seeing the marshal alone. "You'll know where to find us—"

Poke nodded, dismounting to rack his bronc, and Pat turned across to the hotel. Marshal Towner was sitting slumped in a chair in the lobby, puffing a cigar, when he entered. Gif's eyes slitted at sight of him, and the cloud of smoke which obscured his face might have been accidental. Pat wasted no time on greetings.

"No use waitin', Marshal," he started, sliding into the next chair. "Donner didn't bring him in."

Gif's eyes flickered. "Don't miss a trick, do yuh, Stevens?" he growled. "Has it occurred to yuh that this time yuh might be wrong?"

Pat nodded, grinning briefly. "Till I began to think what you'd gain by it," he retorted.

Towner refused to debate the point. "What was your argument with the sheriff?" he countered dryly. Ernie Grapes's name had not been so much as mentioned yet, but he was foremost in both their thoughts.

"I pointed out something he forgot—that he was elected to office, Towner, and you wasn't. Naturally it makes the two of you look at things a bit different—"

"How so?"

"Why, it didn't take Poke long to see that once a rustlin' charge against Grapes was thrown out of court for lack of evidence, it wouldn't make him any more popular."

Towner weighed the bland words carefully. His own voice was flat. "You wouldn't have an eye on Grapes's girl yourself, would yuh, Stevens?"

Pat laughed outright. "You're on a treadmill, Marshal," he tossed back pleasantly. "Frankly, it surprises me to be defendin' old Ernie against you, of all persons—"

"Could be he's makin' his own troubles," was the stubborn answer.

"Not without your help," Pat caught the other up sharply. "You don't seem to appreciate, Towner, that Grapes is under pressure from both sides!"

"Don't see it."

"Then you don't want to . . . Grapes rode with that gang long enough to pry Letty clear, and for no other reason in the world," Pat insisted with heat. "*I* don't have to tell you he's wrapped up in that girl! You took your own advantage of that fact some years back—"

"Go on."

"Well, Towner, if it's news to you, Harve Wells is convinced Letty's crazy about him." Pat omitted to mention recent developments in this regard. "She's his whole interest in that pair."

"So Ern's white as the driven snow, is he? . . . You're

gettin' sentimental now," Gif growled, chewing the cigar. "I'll remind yuh again that I'm after a wolf, Stevens! Whatever I may have t' do, I'll do it!"

Pat made a scornful gesture. "Can't I make you understand? Your stubborn itch to catch Wells can wreck all Ernie Grapes's years of reform, and at his age wipe out his last chance! And what guarantee have you got that it'll work?"

"Oh, come now. A minor rustlin' charge ain't quite that serious. If it'll persuade the old crab to talk, it's well worth the trouble—Poke Donner's trouble, that is." Towner smiled faintly at his weak joke.

"But what if it *should* prove serious?" For the first time Stevens revealed his hunch that the charge of rustling could be dynamite. "Would it make a difference, Towner, if I told yuh exactly what did happen to Rafe Alford's stock?"

"Might."

Pat related the events of Harve Wells's first visit to Grapes's ranch; how the outlaw had urged Ernie to join the gang, believing this would secure the girl for himself—and how the rancher had flatly refused. Then had followed the raid on the Rafter A under Wells's direction, a move deliberately designed to involve Grapes.

"You see how it is," Pat concluded. "Push this ridiculous charge, Towner—and far from closin' in on Wells, you'll be doin' his work."

"Well." By no means sure of his ground, the lawman was thinking hard. "Then I'll make use of the girl, if necessary—"

"But she *is* helping us," inserted Pat swiftly. "Wells is bound to be back for her. And when he comes—bingo!" He spread his hands. "We'll have him!"

Towner gazed absently into space. Inquiries he had made concerning Stevens here in Dutch Springs had altered considerably his opinion of the other. He wanted to believe Pat. But a hundred doubts nagged him.

"This MacEwen that Letty's interested in," he began. "He didn't come back with yuh, did he?"

Pat took the query in stride. "All I can tell you, Towner, is that when Ernie brought the girl home, MacEwen pulled away. He's probably on Wells's trail himself."

"Hunh!" Gif was plainly skeptical. "Why didn't he

plug Harve, the first good chance—or why didn't you, for that matter?'' The point appeared to be the main stumbling-block for him.

"With Harve's friends around every minute?'' Pat's smile was wry. "Talk sense, will yuh? I daresay MacEwen wanted to stay alive, too. I know I did!''

Towner made up his mind swiftly. "So what's our next move, Stevens?''

"Keep your shirt on,'' responded Pat promptly. "I told yuh I want to turn Wells in, dead or alive. I still aim to deliver.''

"Waitin' for him to come to yuh, you mean?'' The marshal's confidence in Letty's fatal attraction was slim.

"As I said before, if you'll let me go about this in my own way—''

"Maybe a deputy's star would help,'' Gif proposed unexpectedly. He thrust a hand in his pocket.

Pat shook his head. "No strings, thanks. I'm not doin' this for money. My own, anyway.''

"Well, I'm persuaded you're in earnest about this, any-how,'' the lawman allowed. He got ready to rise. "I'll be expectin' to hear from yuh, Stevens. And before long.''

"That depends on Wells,'' reminded Pat. "But I think you will. Thanks, Towner, for being reasonable. Old Ernie has trouble seeing things your way—but I'll try to explain.''

"My way!'' scoffed Gif with a sour smile. "Yuh can't see it yourself, boy. I believe yuh could talk the leg off a mule if it was to your advantage!''

Pat left a few minutes later. He did not see Poke Donner again, the sheriff perhaps deciding to leave well enough alone. But he did run into Johnson, his Lazy Mare fore-man, in the Gold Eagle, and the pair put their heads together over ranch affairs. It was late when Pat at last broke away. He decided to remain in town overnight, and after a leisurely breakfast the following morning he started back for Grapes's ranch an hour after sunup.

His talk with Towner had given him plenty to think about and he did not hurry. It was midmorning by the time he began to work up into the hills not far from the Circle G. It was largely by accident that he saw a figure darting across the mouth of a wash.

Alert in a twinkling, Pat circled and closed in, urging his bronc into a dead run. It was never far from his mind that Wells might be spotted here at any time. It was not Harve he had seen, however. Before he got far a man emerged from the brush, rifle in hand, and he recognized Ernie Grapes.

"Keepin' your eyes open, I see." Pat's greeting was brief. "It could be a mistake, though, to go prowling the range alone like this—"

Grapes brushed this aside. "Yuh seen Towner, Stevens?" It was not difficult to determine what was prompting his curiosity.

Pat nodded. "I managed to pound some sense into his head—and I think he'll straighten Donner out." He paused. "Is it only Gif Towner's imagination, Grapes, that you're so dead set against the law?" he asked casually.

"Depends whose brand you're talkin' about." Ernie grew stiff. "Don't tell me Towner's got you askin' yourself questions now!"

Pat waved a hand brusquely. "Towner's all right at bottom, but he's seen too much. Don't blame him for gettin' ideas about you, Ernie, if you refuse to explain anything."

"Don't he know?" blazed the old rawhide. "It's Harve Wells or me. I won't let Letty suffer—but what does the law care? Gif's had plenty o' time to figure that out!"

"Why—" Pat's lips quirked. "I didn't think it necessary to explain to him about that money in the bank. Naturally he's askin' himself just what Harve finds so attractive about Letty . . . Where is she now, by the way?"

"At the ranch with MacEwen, o' course."

"With Brad—?" Pat caught at that.

Ernie nodded. "Seen him sneakin' in soon after I left," he admitted grudgingly.

Pat turned his horse that way. "Donner's visit disturbed her some. I saw that. We'd better relieve her mind."

They climbed the pine-fringed slopes, following the line of least resistance, and at the crest of a minor divide obtained a view in the direction of the Circle G. Old Ernie stiffened in the saddle, his seamed face going tight, as they saw an ominous roll of dirty brown smoke billowing across the swells. It could only come from the ranch.

"Letty—!" gasped Grapes.

"Take it easy. Ez and Sam are guarding those young-sters," exclaimed Pat, seeing his fear. "Something's hap-pened, of course, but it doesn't have to be what you think."

Kicking the horses into a run, they tore forward. It seemed an endless time before they got up where they could see clearly. The sight that met their eyes brought a groan from the rancher. Flames were bursting out of one end of the barn, mingling with the swirling pall of smoke. In a matter of minutes the structure would be nothing less than a blazing pyre.

"No savin' that," Pat yelled above the crackling rumble as they rushed close. "The house is okay so far. But where is everybody?"

Seeking his own answer, Ernie tumbled from the saddle and ran to the kitchen door. "Letty!" He shoved inside, while Pat circled the place in a fruitless search. Reaching the yard again, Pat saw the rancher burst into the open, tragedy written in his face. "She ain't here! There ain't anybody around! They're gone, Stevens. Clean gone!"

Pat slid to the ground. "We haven't looked at that barn yet!"

The words set Grapes into action. Terrific heat poured from the burning barn, but they ran around to the side not yet in flames, shielding their faces with their arms. Cin-ders rained down, stinging their flesh, and the smoke literally choked off their breath. A gust of heat puffed from the yawning doorway as if from a furnace.

Fighting close, they detected shadowy movements against the lurid light. Even as they watched, Sam Sloan came staggering out of the inferno, half dragging and half sup-porting Ezra. Clothes scorched and faces blackened, they resembled spectres. Pat ran forward to help them.

"Great guns!" croaked Ernie, blanching before the sear-ing heat. "Yuh mean you two was in there? Where in God's name are the others, then? *Where's Letty?*"

17.

SAM AND EZRA had watched Pat depart in Sheriff Donner's company with deep misgivings. Neither thought much of Ernie Grapes's chance of escaping the lightning. "Made his mistake years ago," Ez growled. "He's payin' for it now."

Sam was inclined to agree. "Ain't no savin' him this time," he said. "Stevens is smart—but not that smart. Gif Towner'll slap his ears down, come out here, an' take Ernie in tow himself!"

They thought about it gloomily. "Tough on that girl," ventured Ez finally. "Her an' MacEwen stuck their necks out, tryin' t' help the bull-necked old chowderhead. This is their pay—"

"Huh?" Sloan was caught. "What is?"

"MacEwen drove them rustled steers south," pointed out Ezra. "Under orders, o' course. T' save his own hide, Grapes'll tell—an' Brad'll be forced to pull his freight. That leaves Letty t' face Wells alone."

Sam looked alarmed at this. "Why can't MacEwen take her with him?"

"But will he?" Ez was blunt. "Can yuh imagine that perfect gent askin' her t' share an owlhoot's life, runnin' an' hidin'?"

A crafty glint appeared in Sam's normally guileless eyes. "Maybe that could be arranged—" he began.

Once the idea took firm hold of the pair, they lost no time enlarging upon it. Grapes was so upset as the evening wore on that he took no notice of their mysterious whispering. By the time they rolled into bed their plans were perfected. There remained only to await an opportunity to put them into effect.

On the following morning they watched with satisfaction old Ernie's preparations to pull away from the ranch alone. At another time they would have protested vigorously, one of them at least insisting on accompanying him; but now they said nothing. Grapes was scarcely well on his way when the pair disappeared in the barn, leaving the coast clear. It was only a matter of minutes before Sam began to chortle as he watched.

"Here comes MacEwen," he murmured. "We'll let him have a few minutes in the house—"

Brad left his bronc in a safe place, and they lost sight of him altogether till Ez spotted the young fellow slipping around the corner of the house. He tapped at the kitchen window and presently disappeared inside the door.

Waiting impatiently, the partners finally strolled into the yard. Reaching the house, they exchanged a nod and marched purposefully in. Letty and Brad separated hastily as they entered. Sam fixed his eye on them sternly.

"Yuh ready for a ride—I hope?" he brought out flatly.

MacEwen was the first to gather his wits. "Sure, Sloan." He nodded. "I'll go anywheres it seems worth while—"

"We mean the two of yuh." Sam paused to let this sink in. "Fetch your bronc, MacEwen, while Letty gets ready. The sooner we shove off the better."

His authoritative tone allowed no argument. Letty and the young fellow looked at each other uncertainly. "I—suppose we could," the girl conceded somewhat uneasily. "Were you planning to—show us something, Sam?"

"We'll tell yuh about it," Ez cut her off brusquely. "Get your hat, ma'am, or whatever yuh want, an' don't be holdin' us up!"

Letty was ready almost before Sam led her pony up from the barn, and young Brad reappeared at the same moment. "Which way, Ez?" he asked indulgently.

Ez waved a hand vaguely. "Get goin', will yuh? We ain't got all day."

They set off, laboriously climbing a shoulder of the Culebras and striking north. The little hamlet of Gunlock was not much more than a two-hour ride in this direction, a fact which did not escape MacEwen; but he held his tongue until it could no longer be doubted that the isolated supply town was where the disreputable-looking pair were leading them.

"But why Gunlock?" Brad demanded in some mystification. Suddenly he reined in sharply. "Don't tell me you've arranged some kind of a crazy meeting with Harve Wells—?"

"Unh-uh," Sam denied stoutly. "If that was the case, yuh wouldn't've been invited, an' yuh can tie to that!"

"What's up, then?" MacEwen showed signs of turning balky. "Dammit, boys! There's no need of being mysterious—"

Riding close as if by accident, Ez deftly extracted the young fellow's Colt from his holster, and tucked it under his own belt. Brad followed the operation with growing amazement, and Letty looked worried.

"What is this?" rasped MacEwen, backing his horse around to face them. "I never expected a double cross from you two!"

Sam put on an expression of deep disgust. "Can yuh tie that?" he asked Ezra. "Ain't no doin' some folks a favor—"

"Blast it! What *is* there in Gunlock that's so important?" demanded Brad hotly.

"Well—" Sloan looked sly. "I *think* Ed Peterson is still in the justice business. Ed owes us a turn or two—and far as that's concerned, MacEwen, it ain't everybody could persuade me t' officiate at a shotgun weddin'!"

Brad's jaw dropped. He was not sure he had heard aright. "You mean you want—me and Letty to get married?" he barked incredulously. His cheeks flushed as if he suspected a crude joke. "Hang it, Sloan, you've got a hell of a gall!"

For her part, Letty looked at once startled and annoyed. "Just a moment, Brad," she pleaded. "Aren't you a little unsure of your ground? Sam has said nothing of the kind as yet—"

"No? Unless you're plumb addled, you sure know what he means!" retorted Brad vehemently.

"Do I?" Her throat and her face flushed crimson as she gazed at him. Seeing that, Sam began to chuckle.

"Looks like he ain't very willin', Letty," he observed. "Maybe yuh should've picked me—"

Neither paid him any heed, their eyes interlocking. "I don't suppose there's any need to ask whether you'd be willin'," Brad muttered to her. "You've got no reason to think well of me, and I've no right to expect it, either!"

"Brad!" Look and tone were warmly chiding. "Must I spell it out for you—what Ezra and Sam have already seen? . . . I never wanted anything better than to be your wife," she declared bravely. "I've—tried hard enough to make you see!"

With an inarticulate exclamation, Brad crowded his horse close. "You mean that, Letty?" he demanded hoarsely, hope struggling with disbelief in his strained face. "It ain't some kind of a gag? You'd take me—knowin' what yuh do about me?"

Sam and Ez might not have existed for all the notice the engrossed pair gave them now. They had the grace to turn their backs, but they could not help overhearing.

"What do I know, Brad?" The girl sounded breathless.

"I've been a complete fool!" he cried. "Ridin' with crooks—and even lettin' you get mixed up in it! It's all crazy. I should never've allowed it for a minute—"

"And why did you?" she murmured.

"Well, I—" Pausing only briefly, he blurted it out. "It's a long story, Letty. I got acquainted accidentally with Doc—there on the Rafter A range, while we worked together. He seemed to like me. I heard from him how Wells was plannin' to smash Ernie—your dad. I swore I'd block Harve's rotten game on your account—and the only way was to join Harve and watch him. One thing led to another; and blast him, he's ruined *me*—if not all of us!"

"No." She was firm. "Nothing of the kind has happened—yet. Perhaps it's time I took steps to see that nothing does." Resolutely she turned. "Sam. Ezra! Did I understand you to say this—Mr. Peterson, in Gunlock, is a justice?"

"Yeh." Sam smiled at her guilelessly. "Reckon Ed is able t' tie a bona fidey bowline that won't slip—"

Her nod was composed, but happiness made her eyes sparkle. "I think you had better take us to him at once."

"Sure. We'll do that." Ezra's chuckle was sly. "Does seem t' be some question just who's holdin' the shotgun here, though, MacEwen," he remarked dryly. "Maybe it don't matter."

With the big question resolved to his satisfaction, Brad was not to be ribbed successfully, however. "Lay it on thick, Ez." His grin was almost foolish. "I'll get even for this later—if I'm ever lucky enough to do yuh that big a favor!"

Delaying no longer, they rode down into Gunlock, which was nestled deep in the pines. The village was far from large, and they had no trouble locating the man they sought. Ed Peterson, the local J P, was also a storekeeper. Big and blond, he untied his apron as Ezra led him out of his establishment, and eyed the young couple quizzically.

"A little legal business, huh?" he remarked with dry humor. "They both look old enough t' know better. Reckon we needn't inquire about the parents' consent. But knowin' Ez here, it might be prudent to learn if they're both agreeable themselves!"

There could be little question, from the looks on Brad and Letty's faces, that both were as impatient as they were eager. Beaming at them, Peterson nodded.

"Step inside, if yuh will," he directed. "If you've got no serious objections to Ez and Sloan as witnesses, we'll get about this."

The ceremony was brief, marked by Letty's happiness and certainty, and MacEwen's obvious reverence. Insisting afterward on the traditional privilege, Sam laughed at the blushing bride's squirming under contact with his wire-brush stubble.

"Well, Mrs. MacEwen!" observed Ezra as they emerged once more to the street. "Time t' get on home, ain't it, an' start cookin' that weddin' supper?"

"It will be delicious, Ezra," she promised happily. "And I'll expect you to be there."

She was starry-eyed, and her young husband appeared somewhat dazed. Sam regarded them shrewdly.

"Reckon the two of yuh'll be able t' find your way home without help?" he demanded.

They easily reassured him, and a few minutes later set off, having exacted the promise that the partners would presently follow. Watching the pair depart, Sloan shook his head sagely.

"Ain't dead sure that's wise," he grunted. "They'll have t' come down out of the clouds an' wake up t' things all too soon. But maybe it's worth it, givin' 'em a little time t' themselves. They got it comin' to 'em."

He and Ez deliberately lingered about Gunlock for a couple of hours before they remembered the ever-present threat of Harve Wells and took once more to the saddle. Neither would have readily forgiven himself could he have known what was going on at almost the very moment they started back for Grapes's ranch.

Rambling through the peaceful hills, riding close together, Letty and Brad paid small heed to their surroundings. Hand in hand, exchanging vague comments in the intervals of silence, they seemed to be living a dream whose promise neither had been fully confident of seeing realized.

The dream was shattered abruptly as they passed through a scattered, bushy stand of cedar hardly half a mile from the ranch. One moment they were alone; and the next, with a startling rustle of movement, they found themselves surrounded by three stony-eyed men, pushing their horses out of concealment, guns in hand.

"You!" Letty's breath caught sharply as she found herself face to face with Harve Wells.

"Yeh. Me." The outlaw was ominously serene. "Ain't yuh glad to see us—sweetheart?"

Deathly pale, MacEwen noted with leaping dread the wholly unexpected presence of Doc and Chet Denton. The bearded outlaw gave him a cynical glare.

"Do we surprise yuh, Mac?" he murmured, smiling crookedly. "You ought t' know us better than that—"

"What do you want?" the girl said in a small voice.

Harve's harsh guffaw broke the heavy quiet. "Ain't got any idea—have yuh?" he taunted.

It was only too clear to the pair what the purpose of these outlaws must be. Ezra had forgotten to return MacEwen's gun—probably a fortunate circumstance as matters stood. Agonizingly conscious of his empty holster, Brad could only glare his helplessness.

"Pull aside, Wells, and for this once we'll forget we even saw yuh," he said, trying manfully to brazen it out.

"Nice of yuh." As he spoke, Harve coolly forced his horse between them. "Tie him good, boys," he tossed out the careless order. "I'll take charge of this filly!"

Too late Letty attempted to wheel her pony away. He already had an iron grip on her bridle-rein.

"Where are you taking us?" she gasped.

Harve's shrug was callous. "We'll go down and kick Ernie's teeth in, for one thing," he answered brutally. "Is Mac hogtied, boys? . . . Then let's go."

The ride to the ranch was accomplished in nerve-racking silence. MacEwen was too bewildered to ask questions, but he feared the worst. Reaching the ranch yard, Wells glanced around and dismounted.

"Grapes!" he called out roughly. There was no answer, nor did a search of the premises produce the rancher.

"Well, no matter." Harve was grim. "We can afford to wait for the old fool—"

Letty and Brad were hustled into the house and the horses concealed. Coldly businesslike, the outlaws set up a watch. Twice Brad endeavored to start them talking. Doc ruthlessly cuffed him into silence, but Wells was not satisfied.

"Shove the two of 'em in one of these rooms," he growled. "If they make a squawk at the wrong time, yuh know what to do!"

The pair were thrust into another room, where they could only regard each other with worried eyes. It was a bitter wait before they heard excited muttering amongst the outlaws. Minutes of silence ensued, broken abruptly by a racketing scuffle as Ezra and Sam stepped into the kitchen, to be instantly set upon and almost as promptly subdued. They heard Wells cursing roundly as he surveyed his captives.

"You two again?" he roared. "Where *is* that damned Grapes, anyhow?"

"Oh, he's gone." Ez was glib. "Poke Donner picked him up on a rustlin' charge—thanks t' you. Reckon he's in the Dutch Springs calaboose now. Ain't that awful?"

The smack of a slap followed his jibe, and Wells swore

again heartily. This was shortly followed by rumbling murmurs as the outlaws conferred.

Argument broke out as Harve accused Ezra of lying. It was several minutes before the redhead's apparent indifference convinced the outlaw leader.

"Well—we'll leave our callin' card anyhow; and take care of you two at the same time," Harve finally exclaimed harshly. "Get 'em out to the barn, Chet—and Doc, better bring that pair inside. They'll want t' see this!"

Brad and the girl were ushered out in time to see Sam and Ezra being trussed to stanchions in the barn. They failed to understand till Wells climbed to the loft to kick down a quantity of hay. It was piled against the wall in a corner, and Harve methodically dug out a match.

"What are you doing?" Letty screamed at him. "Harve Wells, that's murder—!"

"Oh no." Igniting the hay, Wells glanced slyly at the partners. "If they don't like it, they can walk away—"

"Wells, I'll see you swing for this!" MacEwen shouted furiously.

Doc all but knocked him down, lunging at him heavily; but Harve paused to stare calculatingly at the young fellow. Letty was the first to read his ruthless mind.

"*No!*" she gasped. "You can't throw Brad in the fire like an animal—or, Harve Wells, I'll *never* turn that money over to you!"

Ignoring her, Harve glanced at his confederates. Doc shrugged. Wells cold-bloodedly took time to weigh the matter. "Mac's against us," he pointed out flatly. "His game is mighty plain. By shinin' up to this hussy, he thinks *he'll* get t' spendin' that money, instead of us—"

They nodded stonily. "Better close his mouth anyhow," muttered Denton.

Letty tried wildly to interfere as Doc thrust her husband of a few hours into the barn. Wells whirled her away, hauling her roughly back. Brad himself was set and pale as he was led into a stall and tied, but he was silent.

Already the flames were gathering headway. They draped a corner of the barn, licking out hungrily. Thick smoke hazed the interior, and Doc was coughing as he ran out into the open.

"All right! Let's clear out of this," he barked sharply. "We still ain't finished what we come back for, Harve. Now to get that girl in town t' the bank and make a withdrawal!"

Stunned and in a state of partial collapse, Letty allowed herself to be hurried away.

"MACEWEN IS STILL in that barn, Stevens," croaked Ezra as Pat hauled him and Sam away from the scorching blast. "But there ain't no gettin' him out now—"

"Where's my girl, man?" Grapes almost lifted the red-head off his unsteady feet with the force of his grip. *"Is she in there?"*

"No, no! Wells dragged her off with him after they tied us fellers up an' started the fire," Ez gasped. "Slack off, Grapes! We'll do somethin' about her, if yuh'll let us get our breath."

Pat had waited for no more on learning that Brad was still somewhere in the doomed barn. Leaping that way, he tried repeatedly to reach the gaping door, only to be driven back by the spouting tongues of flame. Rescue was hopeless, and he gave up at last with blackened jaw and eyebrows singed.

"Harve Wells, wasn't it?" he burst out. "He never managed this alone—"

"No, Doc an' Chet Denton come back with him," supplied Sam. "Findin' them hombres must've been what kept him away so long."

"And where in blazes were you two?" Pat barked severely. "I thought you were watchin' things!"

The partners exchanged crestfallen glances. Neither thought it necessary to mention the activities that had taken them away from the ranch.

"It's done now," rebuffed Sam harshly. "Are we chewin' it over—or are we goin' to do somethin' about it?"

"By grab, *I'll* do somethin'!" The wolf in Ernie Grapes became suddenly evident. "I'm goin' after my daughter, an' goin' now!" He started for his horse.

148

Pat turned swiftly to Ezra. "Go along with him, Ez. That's your job, long as he needs a tracker." He waved toward the barn, which was just beginning to go up in good style as the flames burst fiercely through the shake roof. "Sam and I can't leave this while there's any remote chance for MacEwen—not that I think there is," he added thinly. "But maybe with fast action we can save the house."

Ezra glanced back once as he and Grapes mounted the rising hills, to see Stevens and Sloan carrying pails of water toward the house, whose roof was already smoldering under a rain of cinders. Then the one-eyed giant, blackened and gaunt now, swung sternly to his own task.

He had picked up the trail of four horses leading away from the yard. Climbing the bare slopes, the sign looped over the range in the general direction of Dutch Springs. The outlaws could not be any great distance ahead, common sense told them; but they saw nothing, and Ez declined to hurry.

"Come on, come on," Ernie rasped critically more than once. "We're wastin' time here if Wells is headin' for that bank!"

They would have been sadly disappointed had they headed directly for town as he proposed. Five minutes later Ezra pointed out where the outlaws had halted in a group to confer. The horses had stamped here for several moments, and when they pushed on it was to strike straight for the higher hills.

"Changed their minds," the lanky tracker remarked tonelessly. "Could be they're figurin' how t' toll Gif Towner away from Dutch Springs before they move in for the cleanup."

From this point on he stuck closely to the trail, patiently solving every hasty dodge and evasion used by the owlhoots. The way led over the upper ranges, bare now that prudent stockmen had shifted their cattle to winter range far below. The afternoon was waning when Ezra suddenly looked up.

"Gettin' close t' the edge o' Rafe Alford's spread, ain't we?" he growled.

Grapes nodded impatiently. "What of it?"

Ez's single eye was shrewd. "Wells worked the fall

roundup here," he reminded Ernie. "Ten t' one he's makin' for Alford's line camp yonder in the pines."

Twenty minutes later they guardedly scouted the isolated camp through a break in the ragged trees. Sure enough, horses stood before the tumbledown cabin. Dusk made it difficult to determine more from this distance.

Ez insisted on dismounting a good quarter of a mile away. Toting Grapes's battered carbine, he led the way through the scattered pines. Thickening darkness enabled them to spot the flickering campfire in the brushy open space some yards from the cabin. They presently made out the three men seated around the blaze.

"Must be holdin' Letty inside," muttered Ez tensely. "Can I depend on yuh to freeze them hombres, Grapes, while I snake her out o' there?"

Ernie's cold face might have been carved from stone. "I'll make a stab at it," was all he would say.

"I won't lose no time," Ezra promised. "The minute I got her safe, yuh can do as you've a mind to with them rats."

They parted, the big redhead disappearing into the shadows as if he had faded in thin air. Stealing toward the men at the fire, Grapes gave him time enough to reach the cabin. The old rawhide tried to restrain himself, but one clear glimpse of Wells's evil face and he impulsively burst from cover.

"Hoist 'em," he ordered in a curt growl.

They froze in a flash. Harve peered hard in the murky gloom, a look of incredulity on his hard face.

"I'll be danged!" he ripped out, and he began to laugh gutturally. "Why didn't I guess old Ern was bound t' show up, if we only sat still long enough?" His sarcasm was harsh. "Imagine me—tryin' t' coax the old goat!"

The Colt in Grapes's hand cracked, and Wells's hat flew off his head, tumbling wildly. He never moved.

"Still got his fine Italian hand, I see," murmured Doc, bolt upright where he perched with crossed legs. It was evident that the rancher's savagery was no surprise to anyone, and certainly it failed to intimidate them. It was in fact a tactical mistake, warning them that Grapes was their implacable foe, and that this was the showdown. Only cold brass, and the nerve to act on it, could get them out of their totally unexpected dilemma.

"Okay, Grapes. So yuh got us cornered." Denton's bored tone was sinister. "Just what would yuh be after?"

"Ain't no secret," Ernie grated. "I want my girl, an' I aim t' have her!"

"Hunh?" Doc put on an expression of purest surprise. "Letty, yuh mean? . . . Man, you're off on the wrong track," he exclaimed innocently. "Why, we never even seen her!"

He must have calculated that, with three against one, once Ernie could be persuaded to search the tumbledown line cabin they would presently have him at their mercy. The inscrutable mask of Grapes's lined face gave no indication that he sensed the trap.

"I won't argue with yuh," he said, adding the shrewdly expected retort: "She's inside—"

"Nah." Wells began to laugh, smoothly entering into the trick. "Yuh got us all wrong, Ern. Take a look in there if yuh don't believe me." No stranger could have questioned this persuasive tone. "Why, shucks. If you can dig up your girl in that shack, old man, yuh can have her!"

They crouched there, waiting to spring the instant his back was turned. It never came about. There was just then a rasping scrape as the sagging cabin door was thrust back. The outlaw trio's attention jerked to the shack. Into the dim light from the fire stepped the rugged form of Ezra, with Letty at his side. Harve Wells started to his feet in snarling amazement.

"So this is your game, yuh damned old schemer!" he whipped out hoarsely.

As if at a signal, the renegades crashed into action. Tumbling simultaneously backward and sidewise in an effort to get out of the firelight, they clawed at their guns. They fired wildly, lurid flashes stabbing the gloom.

Grapes guessed their strategy. With a cry of fury he sprang forward, concentrating grimly on getting Wells as the outlaws thrashed determinedly to gain the covering brush. Slugs buzzed around him, but he never paused. Sure that he had his bitterest enemy at last, he blasted shot after smoking shot into the ground.

Almost before he had time to realize his failure, a bullet grazed his temple. Another, catching him somewhere in the shoulder, whirled him violently around and dumped him in the dirt, narrowly missing the hot ashes of the fire. Ezra ran forward, his own gun blazing. He scooped Grapes up with a single sweep of his bony arm.

"Get out of the light," he roared. But both were in a fatal position, and slugs whined about them angrily. The big redhead did the only thing he could, and his swinging boot sent the glowing embers flying in every direction.

Old Ernie's unceremonious rescue seemed only to infuriate him. He thrust Ezra violently back. "Get out o' here, yuh big fool!" he bawled. "I told yuh to take Letty away, an' what're yuh doin'?"

Ez didn't argue with him. He dropped to all fours as the owlhoots rose in the brush, yelling to one another.

"Make for that girl!" they heard Wells yell out. "Grab her an' we can still call the turn on this deal!"

Legs crashed through the brush, and Grapes fired at the sounds. His hammer clicked on an empty shell and he plunged to his knees, reloading feverishly. Cruelly hampered by his torn shoulder, he whipped alert as the yelling burst out again.

"She ain't here, Wells!" Chet Denton cried piercingly.

"She's got t' be," thundered Harve. "Beat around, boys! Make it fast! She can't get away!"

"Hell, I tell yuh she's gone!" Doc was equally fierce.

Running this way and that, they argued furiously while Grapes crouched, his ears on the stretch. He had lost all trace of Ezra moments ago, and hope welled in his stout old heart. There was a bare chance the lanky tracker had got away with Letty. Determined to give them all the time he could, Ernie sprang to his feet and unleashed a fusillade in the direction of the searching outlaws.

"That's Grapes," Wells burst out. "He's been hit! He can't get far. Burn the old badger down!"

Guns roared and slugs snarled through the brush as the owlhoots closed in, resolved on a final accounting. Too late Ernie saw his error.

No longer could he hope for any aid from Ezra, who was busy with his own work; and this was a battle Grapes

knew he must fight alone. Ducking and darting, he writhed
through the tripping chapparal; he held his fire now, every
faculty bent on surviving as long as he could. It never
crossed the old rawhide's mind that he could escape. He
merely wanted as many of his foes to go down with him as
he could manage.

Pat and Sam Sloan's fight to preserve old Ernie's home
from the flames, meanwhile, went on. Stevens climbed to
the roof and doused the dry, smoking shakes with pail
after pail of water that a puffing, red-faced Sam handed
hurriedly up to him.

A crisis occurred when, late in the afternoon, the totter-
ing sides of the burning barn crashed in and a volcano of
blazing embers shot high in the air. Pat raced about,
stamping out the tiny flames and slapping at his clothes as
a shower of sparks rained down. For five minutes it was
touch and go; but finally he got the situation in hand and
the worst was over.

Pat climbed down stiffly and sank beside Sam on the
kitchen steps. The barn would burn for another hour, but
at least the ranch house was saved.

"Wells didn't miss," muttered Sam gloomily.

"It's one more score chalked up against him, Sam.
He'll find the price comes high when he settles for
MacEwen."

They moved out toward the barn as the flames died
down. The faces of both were long. The structure was a
total loss, and a sorry tomb for young Brad.

Sam was particularly downcast. "This'll hit Letty hard.
If she ever gets t' hear about it—"

Pat nodded. "But not so hard," he qualified, "as it
would if things had gone much further between them."

"Couldn't go much further." Tersely Sam recounted
the course he and Ezra had taken earlier in the day.
"We're prob'ly responsible for this, gettin' them kids
married off, instead of standin' guard," he confessed sadly.
"It seemed like the right thing t' do at the time."

Pat listened in astonishment. "Well, of all the—!" he
began harshly, then stopped. "We might be able to locate

MacEwen in this mess. At least we can give what's left of
him decent burial.''

The heat died out of the smoldering, smoking barn pit
slowly. The structure had been placed against a slope and
its foundation built up with huge rocks. That left a head-
high space beneath the plank floor, which was reduced
now to ashes. Dusk saw the saddened pair gingerly rolling
the charred beams aside, dodging the billowing ash, and
poking through the debris. Pat even went so far as to drop
down into the pit, picking his way with extreme care.

''Lookin' for something?''

Shock gripped Stevens as he whirled toward the croak-
ing voice.

''Who, me?'' Sloan thrust his head over the edge from
above. But Pat was staring ahead in disbelief.

A boulder two or three feet in diameter had been tumbled out of the barn's foundation and landed in front of a
gaping, rock-enclosed space. In the opening appeared Brad
MacEwen's dirty and disheveled head. He was black and
blistered, his eyes bloodshot and his clothes in tatters. But
he was alive.

''Jumping Judas,'' Pat breathed, automatically pulling
his hat off. ''Don't tell me Wells had you figured wrong,
too!''

''He sure did, Stevens—he ain't begun to find out how
wrong! . . . I got loose in that stall and crawled under a
loose plank. Findin' this cellar was my biggest piece of
luck. But it was awful hot breathin' for a while!''

''What in time yuh talkin' t' yourself about down there?''
Sloan craned over the edge and peered down. His eye fell
on Brad.

''Hey!'' He let out a yell, looking as if he had seen a
ghost. *''Is that MacEwen?''* His round face went fiery red.
''What in hell do yuh mean, scarin' us this way, you
no-good scamp!''

Brad laughed weakly. *''You* was scared!'' he retorted.
''Are yuh gettin' me out of here, or not?''

They went into action swiftly, tearing the hot stones
aside. The worn and exhausted young fellow was presently
lifted out of the hole.

"Get him to the house," said Pat. "He needs a drink and some grub."

MacEwen recovered rapidly. He was scorched and downhearted, but alive. They could not keep him still, however. "Wells has got Letty," he burst out desperately, leaping to his feet. "This is just wastin' time! We got to reach town!"

"Easy, boy. Easy!" Sam urged. "Ain't nothin' t' blow your stack about—"

"Two good men are already on Harve's trail, Brad," Pat interrupted, trying to ease the tension. MacEwen was full of eager questions, and not till he had the whole story did he subside.

The news of Ezra and Ernie Grapes's pursuit of the outlaws quieted him for a time, but he was about ready to break out afresh when they heard hoofbeats.

"Who's that?"

Sam was the first to reach the door, and Pat and Brad followed in haste. They saw Ernie Grapes, one hand clutching his bloody shoulder, almost falling from his bronc.

"Holy smoke! Did yuh run into Wells?" Sam rifled.

"Wells, an' some of his lead, too!" The rancher panted hoarsely. "The skunk shot his way out an' got away!"

Brad sprang forward, shaking him. "Did he take Letty?"

"Ez got her away, boy—I see you made the grade too—"

"Ezra?" MacEwen was electrified. "Where'll he take her, Stevens?"

"I told Ez to get her to town, if possible. Come on! Haul Ernie inside and we'll patch up that shoulder. We've got to be in Dutch Springs in a matter of hours—and blamed few at that. Jump!"

19.

"Hang it, Harve! Yuh sure got tangled up in your own rope with that blasted girl," Doc groused.

"Yeh—too many irons in the fire," Chet seconded. "This is our last deal with you, Wells. We should've let yuh unkink it yourself!"

"Don't give me that! I'm not to blame if you're both lily-livered." Harve was breathing fire. "Yuh both ran when Towner was on our tail—and if yuh hadn't got in another stew about him, we'd be in Dutch Springs now, and that slippery dame with us!"

They were a mile from Alford's line camp, huddled deep in the rocks over a small fire. To their disgust, Ezra had not only succeeded in sneaking away from the line camp with the girl in tow, but in some unaccountable manner Grapes, too, had given them the slip.

"She got away—after we grabbed her for yuh," Doc exclaimed. "All the same, you're comin' up with that money. How yuh goin' about it?"

"I'll get it." Harve's manner verged on insolence. "Soon as yuh get your nerve back we'll start—"

Denton who had been sitting quietly, sprang to his feet. He had had enough of Wells's brand of bullying. "All right, Wells—we'll call your bluff. Here and now. Get on your hocks and take off. We're with yuh!"

"And we expect to end up by handlin' some of that cash," Doc reminded him grimly.

"Don't fret!" Harve's casual bravado was superb. "Letty Grapes ain't the only key to that Dutch Springs bank. It ain't so much but what we can take it apart in a pinch."

"In that case, yuh can take it apart alone," retorted Doc

156

bluntly. "We had the money earned once. We ain't riskin' our necks for it a second time on your account!"

"All right. I can do that too." The outlaw leader avoided his look. "Get the horses, Chet, and we'll ramble."

They struck off down the hills less carefully than usual, although it would have spelled bad luck for anyone who ran into them tonight. Denton rode out on a slope from where he could see the little Circle G.

"Barn's still smolderin'," he reported. Indeed, from this point they could catch the faint odor of smoke on the chilly air. "Reckon the house didn't go, but there's no light there—"

They pushed on past and rode down to the plains. A late moon rose, but they did not hurry. Wells gave no hint of his intended course of action, but finally he drew up in an arroyo on the edge of Dutch Springs and turned to the others.

"Reckon this is safe enough for yuh while I go on in?" he sneered.

Doc scrutinized his face in the gloom. His own lips tightened. "Yeh, it's safe enough, Harve . . . Just don't forget where to find us!"

"If I don't show up by noon, say, yuh can make up your mind I'm still there in town—"

"Oh, we'll find yuh," Chet said significantly.

"If yuh should hear a rumpus any time at all," snapped Wells, "don't hold back on my account."

Without more ado, he rode for the edge of town. Dutch Springs was sprawled out after the manner of most range villages, and boasted the usual complement of scattered outbuildings. Harve found a barn that suited his purpose, and led his horse into an unused stable, then slipped out into the main thoroughfare.

It was still as a graveyard at this hour, and the buildings rose about him, lifeless and dark. He saw no evidence of life, but did not allow himself to become careless on that account. It was approaching dawn, and a ghostly light in the east was strong enough to enable him to make out his surroundings.

Wells gave the place scarcely a glance as he slipped along the wall of the bank. There was nothing to be gained

there before opening time. He stole downstreet in shadow
and gazed long at the Dutch Springs hotel, shrewd specula-
tion in his eye.

"That long-legged galoot probably brought Letty into
town. Ten to one she's right there in that fleatrap—"

Wells knew it might easily prove fatal, however, to
search for the girl without more accurate knowledge. It did
not escape him that in all likelihood Gif Towner was
established somewhere in the hotel. Indeed, the law in all
forms lay in wait for him in this town.

As the sun came up he was forced to abandon the open
street. Taking to an alley, he prowled the littered back-
yards, and found himself presently once more near the
hotel. Although he was convinced that the girl was here,
he could not drag himself away till he knew.

There was a back door to the place, and, crouched
behind a pile of boxes, Harve studied it gloomily. There
were sounds from inside, evidently made by the cook
preparing breakfast, and he was dissuaded from any attempt to enter. But an idea presently came to him. He
waited patiently till he calculated the morning meal was
being served, then rose from his hiding-place and started
boldly for the dining-room window. Men were beginning
to move about in the street, but he must take that chance.

When he reached the window, Harve paused long enough
to study the interior. People were seated at various tables,
and it was only chance that no one noted his shadow at the
window. But—unless she was seated in a corner—Letty
was nowhere among them.

Wells jerked his head back and lost no time in retreating
to cover. He did not fear for himself in this town unless he
ran into the wrong person; but with time his only ally he
was taking no chances. The question was, where to look
next? With almost no hope of locating Letty speedily, he
was at a loose end.

He was crouched in a brushy lot beyond the hotel when
he noticed the cracked and faded sign of the Gold Eagle
across the street. It came over Wells that he could use a
drink now. He tried to put the thought down, but this
glance lingered. Suddenly it occurred to him that bar
clients were few at this early hour; the saloon had in fact

only just opened, and he could see a swamper drearily
sloshing a mop around inside the open door.

He stole toward the street, toward the beckoning swing-
doors, and paused at the edge of the brush to look warily
up and down the street before stepping boldly forth.

Then he saw something out of the corner of his eye that
caused him to stop dead in his tracks. Ezra, the redheaded
tracker with one eye, was jogging up the street astride a
roan. The thud of hoofs came steadily closer, and Harve
shrank down, not daring to risk flight. Had he been seen?
The outlaw lay with bated breath till Ezra jogged on past.
Then Wells sprang to his feet. Letty had last been seen in
this man's company. Surely he must lead the way to her
now!

Ezra dismounted before the hotel and stepped inside,
intending, Harve guessed, to confer with the federal marshal. Wells grasped the opportunity to shift to a safer
vantage point; and it was fortunate for him that he did so,
for Ezra emerged alone a few minutes later and started
away on foot.

Harve watched him head for a comfortable house some
distance beyond the center of town, where Ez knocked on
the door and was presently ushered in. Wells was unable
to decide whose place it might be; but soon Ezra came out,
talked briefly at the door with a stout, elderly woman, then
stalked off.

Abruptly the answer hit Wells. *"That's* where Letty is.
Gave yoreself plumb away that time, bean pole!"

Promptly losing all interest in Ezra, Harve studied the
house. He was in no hurry, and it was not long before he
witnessed the casual departure of a stocky, mustached man
who looked like a merchant, and was in fact Jeb Winter,
proprietor of the general store.

As he lounged in the protection of a shed, Harve coolly
planned his course. It could not be far from time for
opening the bank now. But he had no intention of repeat-
ing the mistake at Antler, where they had barged full into
the rush of opening business. After waiting a while longer,
he started for the house he had been watching, approaching it casually.

Pausing at the door only long enough to make sure no

men were in sight, and finding without surprise that it was locked, he knocked briskly. After a moment steps sounded from within. "Yes—who's there?" came the muffled call. He knocked louder.

The key scraped, and Harve's boot promptly shot into the crack as the door was cautiously opened. A thrust sent it reeling wide. He stepped in, gun in hand, and jammed the door shut to confront an indignant elderly woman.

"Well, I never—!" she gasped. "What do you mean by this?"

"Bring Letty here."

"She isn't—" began Mrs. Winter hotly. But at that moment a hall door opened. The girl stood there, peering curiously. Her eyes widened and her lips moved at sight of Wells, but no words came.

He grinned at her wolfishly. "Expectin' me, was yuh? We'll step down to the bank, girl, and finish our business."

She found her voice at last. "I—have no business with you!"

"You're Harve Wells, aren't you?" Mrs. Winter gathered her scattered forces. "You'd better leave at once, before I call Jeb—"

He did not even look at her. A closet door stood ajar at his elbow. With his free hand he whirled the woman about, thrust her into the dark opening, and forced the door shut on her shrill protests. The key was outside; he turned it. His manner as he faced Letty was wholly businesslike.

"Are yuh ready? Here, grab this shawl." He tossed her one hanging on a hatrack. "All right—move. And just in case you're wonderin', I'd advise no tricks."

She was terrified as she remembered what Wells had already done to her husband. Like an automaton, she twisted the shawl about her head and stumbled out the door. They left the house quietly, shoulder to shoulder, and walked up the side-street.

The bank was on the corner. There was a little-used door at the side, and they paused here. Letty did not need the outlaw's iron hand at her elbow to guide her. The bank was open. He swung the door back, followed her in, and steered her toward a table just inside. Blank checks waited in a rack, and he pulled one out.

"Make it out to cash—and be sure yuh endorse it," he muttered. "You know the amount!"

Letty complied, but her numb fingers made a sorry job of it. Harve snatched up the scrap of paper.

"Okay. Now stay right with me."

Business had been going on for a matter of twenty minutes, and except for one or two people the cashier's wicket was clear. But Wells did not head that way. He stopped and looked about.

Ab Keeler, the bank's president, sat at his desk inside a nearby cubicle, and Harve spotted the unsuspecting official. He tapped lightly on the glass. Rotund and white-haired, Ab looked over his glasses. After glancing around to see whether everyone else was busy, he got up and moved to the door.

"Was there somethin'?" he inquired with a smile.

"Like to see yuh a minute." Wells nodded, forcing Letty into the tiny office ahead of him.

"Sit down." Keeler indicated the chair beside his desk, into which the girl sank as if her legs had deserted her. Ab failed to notice that she avoided his kindly eye. "Now if you'll name your problem," he suggested.

"She wants to cash this." Harve stepped forward and laid the check on the desk.

Putting his glasses back on, Keeler took it up and studied it for a long moment with pursed lips. Running to several thousand dollars, the amount was enough to give any man pause. Rattling the slip in his pudgy fingers, Ab suddenly looked keenly at Letty.

"Seems t' be for the same amount you deposited a week or so ago," he began tentatively.

The girl met his look miserably. She dared not speak. Fearing that she should say the wrong thing, Harve spoke up hurriedly.

"Yes. As it happens, it is."

Ab transferred his alert look to the outlaw's face. To the best of his knowledge, he had never laid eyes on the other before, and Harve's presence here meant nothing in particu-

lar to him now. But with the sixth sense of long experience
he felt something was wrong.

He shook his head, his glance going back to the check.
"I can't cash this," he announced.

"What?" Wells's exclamation informed the banker that
his guess had been correct. "Why not?"

Ab put on a surprised look. "Ain't she told yuh?"

"Didn't ask." Harve's hand whipped out his sixgun.
"Ain't askin' you neither, grandpop. Get the money up!"

Ab never so much as glanced at the gun, but his cheeks
reddened. He had had trouble in the past with headstrong
men, and appeared to believe this was what he had to
contend with now. "Told yuh I can't, didn't I?" he rapped
tartly.

"No?"

"No!" Keeler's jowls quivered indignantly. "She was
in here last night about this money—signed every penny
over to her husband. Control of it is out of her hands. I
dunno who you are, mister, but—"

"Her husband, eh?" Wells knew instantly who this
must be. But he did not betray how this news cut him.
"No matter! We'll let the check go . . . Just reach down
gentle, old boy, and grab one of those coin bags I see in
your desk drawer—" He waggled the menacing barrel of
the Frontier Colt.

The blood deserted Ab's round face in a rush. Letty
started from her chair with a gasp, only to sink back,
shrinking under the grip of Harve's steel fingers.

"What are yuh drivin' at?" the banker cried, livid with
rage.

"Won't be hard. Just step inside the cage there, and
stuff about ten thousand in that sack. Make it mixed bills.
But don't look at nobody, pop, an' *don't say a word*. Just
take it easy! I'll be right here watchin' yuh every second,"
Wells reminded with chilling brevity, "and it might pay to
remember a slug can beat yuh to that vault, or to the
outside door. It will, too!" He stepped close, face ugly.
"Well. What about it?"

Ab looked ready to choke. Coin sack in hand, he tot-
tered to his feet. Watching miserably, Letty saw how bitter
he found the imposed task. It was not for his own safety

that he feared to revolt; but he glimpsed the two girl clerks, and he sighed.

Like a man suddenly ten years older he moved into the cage. Harve watched like a hawk, the gun-muzzle following the banker's every turn. Letty knew he would fire at the slightest excuse, and desperation flooded over her. She would have leaped to thrust the deadly weapon aside, crying an alarm, but Wells stood a full six feet away.

Hands trembling, Keeler fumbled the packets of currency, delaying as long as he could. To his consternation the last customer had finished his business and left. He heard Wells clear his throat. Ab started at the sound. Finishing his task, he turned and started back.

His gun concealed, Harve held the steel gate back for him. He virtually shouldered the banker inside the office, and thrust out a greedy hand. "Thanks," he murmured sardonically, taking possession of the laden sack. "Now if yuh'll just see me to the door—"

Keeler guessed his object. It was the last straw for the paunchy banker. With a bleat of fury, he flailed out at the outlaw's head.

Instantly ready for something of the kind, Harve butted him violently aside, almost toppling him. Shouting a curse, Wells swung the gun up. But this time Letty was ahead of him. She grabbed his arm and tugged sharply just as the weapon exploded with a thunderous roar.

A clerk screamed. Someone knocked over a stool. Wells silently struggled with the girl, yanking to free his arm. She clung like a leech. Harve saw Keeler plunge toward his desk. He knew what was coming if the banker ever reached the gun in his desk drawer. With a bellow, the renegade slammed Letty into the wall and freed himself.

Harve whirled toward the lobby, the sack of money clutched against his side—only to halt dead. In the outer door, like a shade from the grave itself, stood Brad MacEwen, gun in hand.

20.

LEFT TO THEMSELVES, Chet Denton and Doc watched alertly from the arroyo while dawn broke over Powder Valley. They said little as time dragged by. Doc finally growled, "Chet, we're a couple of fools!"

"How do yuh make that out?"

"He ain't comin' back." Doc clipped the words off positively. "Never had any intention to . . . Once he lays hands on that dough, we'll be left holdin' the bag!"

Chet mulled it over for two seconds, his face cold and expressionless. Then he kneed his saddle cinch tight and swung astride. "Maybe we can change his mind," he muttered. "Let's go!"

They made directly for town. There was no sign of Wells's mount as they drew near, and they did not hunt for it.

"Harve won't be far from that bank," remarked Doc tersely.

They headed that way. The building was not hard to identify. They were nearing the place by the side-street, knee to knee, when a yell pierced the silence. A man ran around the corner, stared their way, then bounded back toward cover, his gun slamming.

"It's Gif Towner," Doc cried. "There's that Sloan, too! They must have Harve cornered!" His own gun was out.

Denton reined in and slipped down behind his horse. "We'll settle this right here," he exclaimed. "I ain't runnin' no more!"

Gunshots rang from inside the bank. It told them the outlaw leader was there—apparently in difficulties. Before either could speak, a fusillade swept the street. Denton's horse screamed, gave a wild bound, then thudded into the dust. On the instant Doc's pony spooked. Stung by a slug, it reared straight up. The bearded outlaw slid off, fighting savagely to haul the animal down. Baring its teeth, it shrilled like a mustang. Leaden missiles whistling about his head, Doc abruptly threw the reins away and sprang for the corner of an unharnessed wagon. Chet was already flat behind his prone horse.

"They're figurin' t' burn us, Doc," he called. "Keep an eye peeled there behind yuh—"

Doc bounced lead off the bank corner and grinned mirthlessly across at him. "Wonder if they got Harve?"

The answer came suddenly a moment later. A jingling crash sounded from the side of the bank as Wells himself came tumbling out of a window, glass scattering about him. He had dived through without taking time to open the sash. He picked himself up, and although he showed a slash or two on his arms and a bloody cheek, he appeared otherwise intact. Chet spied the bulky coin sack Harve had somehow managed to retain.

Without a backward look, Wells started to scuttle down the street. "This way, Harve!" Doc called sharply. "We'll cover yuh!"

Wells's grip tightened unconsciously on the bag of currency. He spotted Chet, sprawled behind the dead horse, and picked up Doc over the standing wagon. For an instant he hesitated—and at that moment Marshal Towner, Sam, Ezra and several other men burst into view at the corner. They loosed a blast in the direction of the fleeing outlaw, just as Doc and Denton fired hotly in return. Towner's men ducked, stumbling right and left. Harve took swift advantage of the ensuing lull and dived toward an alley behind the bank.

"Hold on!" Chet bawled after him. "We'll never make this if we don't stick together!"

Wells tossed one contemptuous glance over his shoulder before he ran on. "Hell with you! I pulled this job alone—"

Doc guessed his intent. He whipped his gun around in fury, and sent a slug whining past Harve's face. Before he

could pull the trigger again, Wells had faded from view in a
tangle of sheds and fences.

The outlaw leader had taken time during his early prowling to look the ground over and was making now for his
bronc by the shortest possible route. An expression of cold
amusement flitted over his face as he thought of Chet and
Doc, pinned back there in the street by the marshal's
posse.

"They wasn't figurin' on givin' me time for this!"

He meant to abandon them callously to their fate, and to
make sure of his own skin. Unfortunately for him, there
were others who knew Dutch Springs as well as he. He
had covered hardly more than a hundred yards when a gun
cracked to his left. A slug nicked his arm, making him
almost drop the sack. Wells whipped a shot back without
aiming, and swung the other way.

"Come back here!" he heard Ezra bellow.

A rifle crashed, this time directly ahead, and Harve saw
Sam Sloan at the corner of a shed, hastily levering in
another shell. The outlaw swerved away, racing at a mad
pace, and finally lost sight of Sam.

His face was strained and deadly. "They're tryin' t' cut
me off," he gasped. "Maybe I can reach another horse
somewheres—"

But he saw none. Main Street, where his chance of a
mount might have been good, was an impossible distance
away. Wells halted briefly, sucking air into his aching
lungs, to size up his situation. This proved a mistake.
Again Ezra fired, pelting after his quarry; again the slug
droned so close that it made Harve jump.

He burst across a warehouse yard, but wagons, boxes
and barrels barred his way. There was a narrow gap leading toward the front and he made for it. He had barely
reached the open when there came a slap of boots, and
Brad MacEwen appeared directly before him, leaping
forward.

"I missed the first time!" cried Brad. "I've got yuh
now!"

His gun swept up. Whatever he may have expected, he
was in for a shock, for Wells charged squarely at him.

They crashed together, and Brad's Colt went off harm-lessly into the air. He was knocked cold, and the outlaw ran squarely over him.

Wells darted across the beaten lane in front of the warehouse, leaped a low fence and dived into the brush. He could see the barn now where his horse waited. He cursed the wariness which had persuaded him to leave it so far away, then sprawled down on all fours as a rattle of firing broke out somewhere behind him. Panting like a hare, he hugged cover and waited.

Boots clattered in the lane and he heard yelling. "He came this way!" Ezra cried harshly. "I seen him!"

"Dang it, Ez—that was *me* yuh blame near shot!" Sam Sloan hurled back. "Can't I beat nothin' into your head? He turned that way!"

They quarreled excitedly for a moment and ran on. Wells did not delay. Gathering himself, he made sure the coast was clear and ran, bent over, toward the barn.

As he reached it and forged along the weathered rear wall the crackle of distant gunfire calmed his immediate fears. A rusty-hinged slab door gave way to his tugging. He slid into the shadowy interior.

"Made it!" he panted. "I fooled the whole—passel of dunces. With one leg over that bronc—this thing is licked!"

His flight had taken its toll, however, and his breath came in gasps. Stumbling into the main wing of the barn, he hurried toward the stall. His horse nickered and stamped. Another time Wells might have noted its nervousness; but haste pressed him too cruelly now. He took a moment to stuff the money sack into a saddlebag, cursing its tight-ness. Then, toeing the stirrup, reins in hand, he started to swing astride.

"Hold it, Wells!"

Harve knew that hated voice. He realized that Pat Ste-vens was somewhere directly behind him, crouching in the shadows, with gun trained. Stevens had patiently bided his time, choosing this awkward moment to make his play.

Wells acted in a flash. He dropped to the straw-littered floor beside the dancing horse, squirming over like a cat as his hand streaked to his gun.

The crash of Pat's Colt echoed through the stall and the bullet smashed through the outlaw's chest. Harve writhed, soundless. Although mortally hit, somehow he found his knees. The gun had jarred from his grasp, but he recovered it, fumbling it with both hands. His effort, as he strove to bring the barrel up, was terrible. Then, just as his next bullet tore the planks between Pat's feet Harve Wells slumped, dead.

Pat wiped his forehead with a palm, and jostled the body gently with a toe. "Whew!" he whistled, leaning against the stall. "One of those hombres that gives up hard."

It took a moment to calm the excited horse. Heaving Wells up, Pat lifted him across his saddle, head down, legs jutting and arms swinging limp. Taking the animal by its headstall, he led it into the open. Without a pause he started for the bank.

Excitement there was general, and scores of men milled about the corner now that the shooting had ceased. A man on the edge of the crowd let out a cry when he glimpsed the burden on the horse behind Pat, and others turned to stare.

Poke Donner, the Powder County sheriff, broke through. "Who *is* that yuh got there, Stevens?" he croaked sharply. "It—it ain't—?"

Pat's nod was curt. "That's *just* who it is, Donner. Harve Wells—in person!"

"Well. Makin' delivery, are yuh, Stevens—accordin' t' contract." Marshal Towner's tone was wooden. "It happens that Wells got away just now with around ten thousand of the bank's money—"

"Take a look in his saddlebag, Gif." Pat was equally stolid. "I don't think he spent any of it."

The money was found intact, still in the sack into which Ab Keeler had stuffed it. Ezra and Sam came hurrying up as the agitated banker completed a brief examination.

"Well, boy!" Ez slapped Pat resoundingly on the back. "Nabbed the skunk without our help, didn't yuh?" There was reproach mingled with his honest envy.

"No," Pat contradicted warmly. "On the contrary, Ez,

you and Sam flushed him my way—and Wells did the rest. There's no arguin' with his kind!''

A man laughed, but the sound was drowned out by a fresh disturbance. They turned to see grim-faced Ernie Grapes herding Doc and Chet Denton forward. The scowling outlaws were much the worse for wear.

"Here's your Rafter A rustlers, Donner," Grapes growled crustily at the goggle-eyed sheriff. "Go at it right, an' these hombres'll explain anything yuh don't understand—"

Pat nodded confirmation. "I watched those birds in operation, Sheriff," he added. "I'm free to talk now."

"That's fine," Gif Towner broke in heavily. "But hold on here. There's another member of this crowd that ain't accounted for at all—"

"Gila, yuh mean." Sam spoke up quickly. He began to laugh. "Yuh'll find him at that place near Canyon, Marshal. But take a shovel along. Gila's another smart hombre that ran into a little difficulty with Stevens!"

Towner's shaggy brows cocked inquiringly.

"He's right, Marshal. I won't say the man's six feet under—they were a little hurried that day—but he's out of sight. And with these handsome birds"—Pat gestured toward the crestfallen captives—"I expect that washes up the gang."

"Does, does it?" The federal lawman looked around. He had noticed Brad MacEwen only a moment ago, hurrying through the front door of the bank. "There's a gent inside I'm honin' for a word with!"

Pat read his thought and started to accompany Towner, gesturing to Ernie Grapes to follow. They found old Ab planted in the doorway. The banker halted them with upraised hand.

"Yuh can't go in there now," he ruled, his snowy mustache bristling with secret importance.

"Why can't we?" Gif rumbled, forcing his way past in spite of Ab's indignant protests. Pat saw the banker's meaning as his eye fell on MacEwen and Letty in each other's arms. He suppressed a chuckle, and followed Towner straight for the young fellow.

Hearing their voices, Brad turned away from the girl,

and his face fell. He knew what to expect. Stevens was the first to get a word in.

"Towner, I want you to meet Brad MacEwen. He was partly responsible for drivin' Harve Wells my way, out there—and got a lump on his head for his pains. But mainly," he added casually, "Brad came in to turn over the whole amount of Wells's robberies . . . That," was his significant comment, "ought to speak for itself."

Towner accepted this astonishing news dourly. "It'll go a long ways, anyhow—if true."

"Yuh needn't question that," put in Ab stiffly. "He's got the amount to his credit, right here in my bank."

Gif stared at the young fellow blankly. "What kind of a rabbit's foot are yuh carryin', boy?" he demanded. "Ezra told me last night yuh went up in smoke, there at Grapes's ranch!"

"It ain't Wells's fault if he didn't," said the big red-head, who had just entered with Sloan. "He was in that barn all right, Towner. Stevens an' Sam dug him out of the foundation after the fire died down."

"Sort o' gettin' in on the ground floor, yuh might say," Sam grinned. "That's all squared now." He sobered swiftly then. "But Jumpin' Jehosophat, Stevens! Yuh went an' wiped out the best part o' Wells's gang before they coughed up. Are yuh forgettin' our horse money?"

Pat put his mind at rest on that score. "MacEwen here is prepared to hand you the full amount, soon as he finishes his business with the marshal."

"I'll take care of that right now," Keeler seconded promptly. "I reckon MacEwen's ready and willin' . . . Everybody owes that young lady a debt for playin' her hand so smart; but I don't hanker to keep stolen money in this bank any longer than I can help!"

Silently, Marshal Towner followed every detail of the final accounting. As the banker prepared drafts covering the various amounts named by the lawman, and every penny appeared to be accounted for, Towner pondered.

"Blast it, MacEwen. I dunno about you," he rumbled gruffly as Brad signed over the last remittance with a sigh of relief. "Way yuh act, a person would take yuh for a plumb honest hombre!"

At MacEwen's side now, her face strained, Letty confronted the federal marshal squarely. "After this, I should hope you'll not take him for anything else, Mr. Towner!" she exclaimed stoutly.

Gif shook his head stubbornly. "*He* knows, and you know, he's been seen in places where he'd no right to be, ma'am . . . I won't mention Antler by name," he drawled, "but yuh get my meanin'."

They did. All those really concerned for the young puncher had been waiting uneasily for this moment. MacEwen's participation in the Antler bank robbery was indisputable. Pat at least had hoped to circle around the fact. But it was not to be. Towner's duty was plain if he chose to follow it to the letter. Brad himself was the first to recognize this.

"All right, Marshal." He spoke up resignedly. "I won't give you no trouble. What'll you do with me?"

"Well." Gif was plainly perplexed. "I can take yuh in, of course—"

MacEwen nodded dejectedly. "You can do that. My wife will be waiting when I come out, if it's fifty years. That's one thing I can be sure of."

Towner's eyes widened. "Your wife! . . . Are you two *married?*" The look on Letty's wistful face was answer enough. "Damn!" the marshal exclaimed under his breath. He stared at Brad in well-simulated anger. "You young rip! Manage to stay one jump ahead of me all the way, don't yuh?"

"Mr. Towner!" Intuition wrenched a cry of joy from Letty. "What do you mean—?"

He regarded her dourly. "It means I'm parolin' MacEwen in the custody of Ernie Grapes, young woman. He better mind his manners, too!" He cleared his throat. "Yuh hear that, Ern?"

Grapes nodded. He could be silent in his own right; but his old heart thudded warmly in recognition of the lawman's final endorsement—it was compensation and more for all the rancher had endured.

Pat and the partners followed all this with sly smiles.

"What you're doin', o' course," remarked Sam mischievously, "is supplyin' Ernie with a top ranch hand at the cheapest rate goin'. Not that I'd accuse Grapes of plannin' it that way—"

Gif glanced at the rancher, a twinkle in his eye. "What about that, Ern?"

"Well." Ernie was deliberate, yet none missed the shadow of a wink at his smiling daughter. "It's like this, Towner. I had to make somethin' besides an outlaw out of Mac, on Letty's account," he confessed dryly. "So I settled for makin' an in-law out of him!"